NO PEACE IN OUR TIME
By David Miller, Captain (Submarines) US Navy (Retired)

D1521875

Dedication

I especially want to thank the female members of my Duke University, FUQUA School of Business, Class of 1994. As I watched and worked with these women during my two years at Duke, they inspired me. They allowed me to realize that the Navy's exclusion of women on submarines was the result of a terrible lack of vision and failure to get the best people to staff these fantastic warships. I am happy to say that the Navy is now getting superb women from the US Naval Academy and their ROTC programs. This will improve a critical element that is daily at the tip of the military and diplomat spear that protects our country.

Preface

No Peace in Our Time is a work of fiction and all the characters and adventures involving Drake Chandler, his crew on the Pittsburgh and the military and national command authorities are imaginary. But I have attempted to portray the operations and capabilities of United States nuclear submarines, especially as they introduced women into their ranks, accurately for the reader. Keep in mind that hope, fear, and passion are key elements to any great story and I certainly took liberties with my characters in this novel.

I originally wrote it as a screenplay more than five years ago: a screenplay that was never going to be made into a movie, but it is a great story that I felt millions of readers would enjoy. It is written at a time when women were just entering the submarine force, something that should have happened many years earlier. It involves realistic men and women, in the real world of submarine operations, thrust into the no-win position of serving international diplomacy while protecting the United States against a nuclear attack. It contains details of interpersonal politics like those of any large organization where jealousies and intrigue sometimes get in the way of doing what is right.

It is also a story filled with details of everyday submarine life that many of my fellow submariners will remember with pride and my non-submarine readers will find interesting. It is a fictional story, but I wanted to incorporate a sense of realism that reflects the real world of how 120 men and women would operate a nuclear-powered warship in Harm's Way. Some may find the dialogue a bit stilted, but when you are making routine decisions in a dangerous environment that could affect the safety of everyone on board, there is a preciseness in the way professional men and women speak. There can be no confusion when operating nuclear power plants, operating systems under dangerous underwater conditions or shooting war shot weapons.

There may be things that might confuse some readers who do not have a submarine or Navy background. I wanted the story to be realistic in showing what really happens in interactions among a submarine commanding officer, his executive officer (XO), his chief of the boat (COB), and his officers and crew. To do that, nuclear submarine jargon needs to be used.

The concept of one's rank and position is always confusing in Navy stories. You will read about commanding officers of submarines sometimes called "Captain" because Navy tradition dictates that an officer in charge of a vessel is referred to as "Captain," even if he is an enlisted man or woman. On some occasions, you will hear these men and women referred to with their actual Navy rank, which on most submarines is a Navy commander. The other confusing position is that of a commodore. This is a senior Navy captain who oversees a group of ships or vessels. There are two in my story, and my protagonist, Drake Chandler, will operate under both, but only one at a time.

The other confusing point for many with be the concept of a submarine's control area. This is the area of the ship where the officer of the deck, the officer in charge of the ship's operations, oversees the Ship's Control Party, Fire Control, and Navigation personnel executing their duties. It contains most of the sensor-processing displays and/or communication systems with those who monitor the sensors or other parts of the ship. The submarine control area includes the conn area where the traditional

4

submarine periscopes are manned and many of the critical sensors are displayed. On the USS Illinois in my story, a Virginia Class Block III submarine, the periscopes are actually externally mounted raised cameras. The conn is where the officer of the deck spends most of his or her time when submerged. There is also the ship's control station within Control. This is where the diving officer of the watch directs the position of the sail planes and stern planes, as well as the flooding of water in and pumping of water into and out of the ship to maintain ordered depth. When the ship goes to "battle stations," the control room is then called the "attack center."

I hope I didn't confuse you too much. I think if you hang in there, you will quickly become engrossed in the efforts of Drake Chandler to prevent World War III.

Prologue

President Lincoln Jefferson looked out the window in his small office as Air Force One took its craftily planned victory lap around Washington, D.C. The plane's approach was being televised all over the world. In the orange sun of twilight, it was the stuff the press loved. It seemed the media always stood up, rolled over or played dead at his command. They wanted access to the Jefferson White House, the perks it brought and their elevated status in the industry.

He had needed them for this trip, and it paid off well. They beat down his opponents in Congress and belittled the radio talking heads, especially those at Fox News. They were a key to his success with North Korea's Kim Il Un, as he used his best skills to convince Kim to dismantle his nuclear weapons program and move North Korea toward a more stable position in the world of nations.

The child of a crack-addicted mother who got impregnated by a Ugandan war lord's son, Lincoln had been raised by his maternal grandparents after his mother died of a drug overdose and his father renounced his son and left the country. His grandparents sent him to very good Catholic and private schools, where his background allowed them to get scholarships to defray the cost. There was no way they were letting their grandson attend the same public schools that had failed their daughter.

He was an affable child in school and found he was able to bring people together and rally behind his positions on difficult issues. When things did not go his way, he knew how to use his background and difficult upbringing to shame them into backing down, a technique that had served him well since. Starting in his upscale high school, then Columbia University and finally at Harvard Law School, Lincoln Jefferson was the best at using his smooth-talking persona to bring bickering factions together. They all knew the consequences of not complying with his wishes.

Susan Grains sat in the president's conference room, going over the draft of a United Nations Security Council resolution to implement the commitments agreed to under the North Korean nuclear deal. For a moment, she remembered when she was in the Political Science Department at Harvard. She had been just starting out in a group of old white guys who had no concept of progressiveness and clung to the old ways. They had tried to control her, but her ambition outfoxed them as she got herself appointed to highly visible committees and study groups. Her around-the-clock relentless efforts were quickly recognized, and she soon blew off her research requirements. She smiled when she remembered the tenured staff trying to get rid of her, and the university president, under pressure from the Democratic Party, overrode them, leaving them all with egg on their faces.

Back to reality, she realized that once the resolution passed in the U.N. General Assembly, there was nothing Congress could do. This was the most fun part of her job; giving Congress another stick in the eye was a hoot. The flailing following the Iranian nuclear deal was comical as the Republicans and many in the military tried to stop the agreement. But using the U.N. was icing on the cake. The Republicans had no sense of global cooperation and diplomacy. They were still stuck in the past, not recognizing that the United States could no longer dictate what went on in the world. They obviously had never read her thesis and the many papers that had elevated her to the height of academia and onto the president's staff as National Security Advisor.

The door opened and President Jefferson entered. He saw his favorite cunning smile on her face. Susan Grains was his attack dog, with no scruples when it came to achieving her goals. He had heard when she was in competition with some guy for the law review at Yale, she had broken into his house and sabotaged his application and deleted all his other files.

"Susan, how's it looking?"

"Great sir. The echo chamber has all the press lapping up our spin and the opponents can't get a word in edgewise – except for the assholes at Fox News."

Lincoln smiled and gave her a tough look. "I want no backing down on this. We drive this to completion and we're taking no prisoners."

Susan chuckled. "Sir, taking no prisoners is never a problem for me."

Later, looking into the mirror in his bed chamber, President Jefferson adjusted his tie in preparation for meeting his loyal supporters. The Air Force staff on Air Force One was perfectly recruited to meet his needs. Captain Lydia Criten was not only beautiful, she was a tiger in bed compared with his holier-than-thou wife, Bianca. Lydia came out of the bathroom adjusting her skirt and putting on her jacket.

"Lydia, you are one hell of a relaxation asset. I sometimes worry I get too tense."

Lydia moved in to make the final adjustments on the president's tie. "Sir, it was all my pleasure."

Air Force One had finished its final approach to Andrews Air Force Base, landed, taxied, and stopped. The president's accommodation ladder was strategically arranged to allow Jefferson to come right down to a podium with the presidential seal. Hundreds of cameras and reporters were all waiting for the triumphant president. All of the staff had debarked and now waited for the president to come down the ladder and speak.

CNN reporter Ted James was set up to cover the president's return. "Wolf, the president triumphantly returns from discussions with North Korea's Kim Il Un, where he successfully got the North Korean leader to stop production of nuclear weapons.

"The excitement here is electric," he gushed. "On the tarmac, hundreds of supporters surround a podium and teleprompter. Behind it, the president's closest staff members and traveling entourage who had accompanied him to North Korea are standing. As the president exited the plane and waved from the top of the stairs, the crowd cheered wildly. The president jauntily walked down the stairs and moved to the podium. President Jefferson is in his element. He is ready to give his remarks."

Lincoln Jefferson stood behind the podium, listening to the cheering as he waved. Finally, the moment was right.

"Thank you. Thank you. I return to the United States with great news for the American people and the world. I have achieved a next step of my 'Peace in Our Time Initiative' with the removal of the nuclear weapons threat from North Korea. In my discussions with North Korea's leader Kim Il Un, he agreed to stop his nuclear weapons program and destroy his current stockpile of nuclear weapons material in exchange for aid from the United States. I cannot take all the credit for this achievement. Our Chinese, Russian and other Asian friends were key in these negotiations. I look forward to expanding on my achievements with Congress and the American people, but right now I want to

go home and see my family. God bless America."
    As the crowd cheered, President Jefferson waved and
moved off to his limo.
    Ted James, with a small tear in his eye, resumed his report.
"Wolf, this is no doubt the greatest triumph for any president. But,
as much as the president is exuberant in his success, there are
many on Capitol Hill and at the Pentagon who have grave
misgivings. They are upset over his plan to bypass Congress and
use a U.N. Security Council Resolution as the authority for his
actions, just like he did on the Iran nuclear agreement.
Additionally, they strongly disagree with him for agreeing to
remove the U.S. Navy Ballistic Missile Defense cruisers and
destroyers who provide the defense against any North Korean
nuclear weapons launches and monitor North Korean
communications and movements for years. We understand that the
commander of U.S. Forces Pacific, the commandant of the Marine
Corps and the director of the Missile Defense Agency have
resigned their posts in protest of the North Korean agreement.
Time will tell, but there is euphoria in the air. I tell you, when I
hear President Jefferson speak, I get this thrill going down my leg.
I don't have that feeling too often. This is a great day for
America."
    As the president departed, his entourage left the area
around the podium, except for Susan Grains, her assistant,
Michelle Pak, and Mr. Jong Song-taek, prime minister of the
North Korean cabinet. Mr. Song, as he was known, was a
longtime friend and confidant of Supreme Leader Kim Il Un, and
critical to the negotiations in the Peace in Our Time agreement.
    Susan leaned in and spoke. "We have done well together.
We overcame the many objections from both sides in a spirit of
cooperation that will serve us both well."

Song smiled, realizing he had done his job well. "Yes, Susan we made a great team. We must stay in close contact. The supreme leader will have little difficulty dealing with his detractors, but your Congress and military are a different story. You must get them under control."

As Karen departed, Mr. Song watched her leave, then whispered in Michelle's ear. "Your parents and sister are safe for now. You've done well. Don't disappoint me."

PART ONE – THE TACTICAL READINESS EVALUATION
Chapter 1

As USS Pittsburgh, 688 class submarine and the "Pride of the Steel City," glided on the ocean's surface, the sounds of water rushing over the main deck and past the sail gave sort of a musical rhythm to the atmosphere. The warm sun beat down with a blinding sheer coming over the mountains of Guam and reflecting off the eastern ocean surface. Commander Drake Chandler, commanding officer of USS Pittsburgh, sat on the top of the sail at the back of the bridge cockpit. He looked back toward the harbor mouth, where the shape of a tug was visible on the horizon, returning to Guam after dropping off the Tactical Readiness Evaluation Team about thirty minutes earlier.

Drake had been in command of Pittsburgh for more than four years. He had assumed command of a pretty good ship and made it the best in the Pacific Fleet. That success resulted from his ability to pick the right people and do the right thing, even when it meant challenging the status quo protocols of this squadron and the force commander. Until the recent arrival of the new squadron commander, Drake had been the number one submarine commander in the Pacific Fleet.

The new commander of Submarine Squadron Fifteen was Navy Captain Stephan Sails, who was the son-in-law of the former undersecretary of the Navy. Drake had exposed the undersecretary for falsifying test data to stop the development of the Navy's submarine-launched Anti-Ballistic Missile system. It cost the undersecretary his job and he was being prosecuted until the president shut down the effort.

Directly in front of and below Drake, Lieutenant Carla Kelly, the ship's officer of the deck and weapons officer, along with her two lookouts, watched as Pittsburgh transited to the diving point for its first at-sea tactical readiness evaluation in more than five years.

Drake wore a warm smile. His Pittsburgh was finally being given a chance to show what she could do at sea. Fifteen years ago, Pittsburgh had been held up in the shipyard for seven years, right after she was refueled. All her 688 class submarine sisters had long ago run of out fuel and were decommissioned. She was old, and the last of the 688 class submarines, but with a full load of fuel, she was still a capable fighting ship with many years of operations left.

Now that the new Virginia class submarines were coming off the line and the modern 688 Improved submarines were operating, her aged one-of-kind fire control and sonar systems were no longer being updated due to cost. At-sea TREs were expensive, so now the evaluations were done in onshore trainers. As a result, when Drake's crew's tactical readiness had to be evaluated, it was done with attack trainers where the systems were nothing like Pittsburgh's ancient configuration. That always ended up in Pittsburgh being evaluated as below average.

Drake Chandler had finally worn down the Force commander to let him demonstrate his ship's tactical readiness by going one-on-one against another submarine at sea. He was surprised at how easy that was, but today he would be going against the newest of the Virginia Class submarine USS Illinois. Illinois was a Block III Virginia class with the latest and greatest in sonar sensors, fire control systems, weapons and, most important, sound quieting. Virginia Block IIIs were literally black holes in the ocean. Everyone knew Illinois was going to clean house on Pittsburgh, but Drake knew in his heart that fighting a ship is far more than the latest and greatest technology and electronics. It took a crew of men and women who thoroughly understand their ship and systems and knew how to use them.

Carla Kelly looked back at Drake. "Captain, it's great to be at sea again and actually get a chance to show what we can do."

Drake nodded approvingly, looking over the side.

Carla continued, "Captain Prudsen was a bit less than friendly when he was up here after boarding. Is there something I don't know?"

Drake shook his head. "You know all you need to know, Lieutenant. You just get us submerged on time."

Drake chuckled to himself. He rarely referred to Carla Kelly as "Lieutenant." She was one of the best young officers with whom he had ever served – smart, aggressive, and demanding, but with empathy. Right now, Drake thought she needed a little humility.

From below came an announcement. "Officer of the Deck, the ship is rigged for dive with the exception of the Bridge."

Carla responded with, "Very well."

Drake scooted forward, dropping down into the conn area and calling out, "Officer of the deck, I'm going below. Be smart about diving – it's part of the evaluation."

Carla gave him a frustrated look and rolled her eyes like a child at an overbearing parent. "Yes, sir."

The TRE brief was being held in the wardroom, which was in the middle, the second of three levels. It was the compartment where officers had their meals, and was the major meeting room where planning, training, briefings, and officer qualification boards were held, and was sometimes a place for junior officers to relax. The officer staterooms were directly in front of the wardroom and its small pantry, where the culinary specialists prepared meals from the ship's galley for the officers. At that moment, the CSs were providing a coffee service to the TRE team and the Pittsburgh's key tactical weapons personnel.

The captain's chair was at the head of the table. No one else, not even admirals, sat there. Seated to the left of the captain's chair was the TRE senior officer, Captain Jerry Prudsen, who was the squadron chief staff officer and a major Drake Chandler and USS Pittsburgh hater.

Prudsen had been the executive officer on the Maryland when Drake was squadron engineer. During a major internal nuclear boiler inspection, he, his engineer, and captain had left the ship for a weekend of drinking and other mischief. When a nut had accidently dropped into the boiler, the system had to be drained to retrieve it, requiring a complex and delicate realignment of the nuclear reactor and support systems to support the difficult operation. None of the ship's senior officers could be found, so Drake Chandler stood in for them as a senior watch officer. His commanding officer had almost been fired for this, and Jerry Prudsen failed to make command. During the investigation and non-judicial punishment, Drake Chandler was the main witness against him. Now it was time for payback. To the left of Captain Prudsen was his evaluation team.

Lieutenant Commander Karen Young, the ship's executive officer, sat across from Prudsen in her designated XO position to the right of the captain's chair. Carla Kelly, the weapons officer, along with the ship's navigator and the engineer filled out the rest of the seats on that side. The chief of the boat, Master Chief Sonar Technician Mike Riner, stood at the table with Radioman Chief Rita Belt, Corpsman Amanda Rothlein and the communicator, Lt.

Mike Conklin. On the table was a large chart of the ComNavMarianas North-South Undersea Test Range to the west of Apra Harbor.

Karen Young was another on Jerry Prudsen's most despised list, not only because she was a female and out of Purdue no less, but because she had destroyed his best friend Bobby Ester's career when he was in command of the USS Pennsylvania. She had been engineering officer and had refused to sign off on a procedure to bypass critical steps on a test of a sub-safe system. Ester overrode her objection and ordered the test anyway, resulting in severe damage to the ship. Bobby was relieved of command for cause. But even though Young was regarded as a hero, her career was damaged. As in all major organizations, when things go bad, everyone in the wake of the corrective action is tainted. Karen was sent to a submarine systems coordinator job at Raytheon Missile Systems in St. Louis, Missouri. That should have ended her career, until fucking Chandler bypassed everybody and got her assigned as his XO.

Lieutenant Kelly was another story. A hot running nuke out of the academy, she had been assigned to the SSGN Florida, guided-missile submarine. She was everybody's pick to be the Navy's next poster girl. An aggressive black girl from Mississippi with movie star looks and charisma, she had been an all-American swimmer and Trident Scholar at the Naval Academy, but she pissed off the naval hierarchy when she refused to take an assignment as the Vice-CNO's aide after her first tour on Florida. When she was caught on social media commenting that she didn't want to be some white admiral's diversity girl, but wanted to prove herself at sea, that was it for her career. They dumped her at the Bangor Washington Trident Refit Facility's Undersea Vehicle detachment at the Submarine Development Squadron.

But Carla Kelly was good no matter where she went. Her accomplishments at the Unmanned Undersea Vehicles detachment recovered her career and then Chandler used the same technique of bypassing the chain of command to get her on Pittsburgh.

Drake Chandler entered and everyone, but Captain Prudsen stood. Drake looked at Jerry, then waved them all to sit. Looking less than enthusiastic, he opened his briefing folder.

"I'd like to welcome Captain Prudsen and the Tactical Readiness Evaluation Team aboard Pittsburgh, the oldest and still very capable U.S. Navy nuclear submarine. I assume the XO has seen to your administrative needs?"

Jerry Prudsen rolled his eyes and spoke mockingly. "Yes, they have been quite accommodating. But let's get to the TRE brief."

Drake knew the less-than-friendly tone in Prudsen's voice didn't bode well for Pittsburgh.

Jerry continued, "As you know, we have not done at at-sea TREs for many years due to cost constraints, and now your complaining to the force commander has somehow resulted in us having to conduct this ridiculous TRE on the Navy's oldest submarine – one that should have been decommissioned years ago."

Drake smiled. "So glad to see you are in a good mood as we prepare to start."

From down the table, Carla could not hold back her animosity. "Captain Prudsen, sir, this is only fair given that there are no shore-based attack center trainers that have Pittsburgh's fire control and sonar systems. Making us go one-on-one against another submarine crew in a shore-based trainer using their systems guarantees, we lose."

Drake looked sternly at Carla and gave his crew members

a challenging eye. "Weps, stand down!" Looking at Jerry, he added, "Captain Prudsen, you know we are old only because of the delay caused by a shipyard fire fifteen years ago. But that is how it is, and we're not going to change that. We just want a fair shake. Please continue."

Jerry Prudsen smirked. "Thank you. As I was saying, we have not done a TRE like this for years." He stood and pointed to the chart on the table. "You and Illinois will be on the range at the same time. Illinois is depth zone shallow and Pittsburgh is depth zone deep. There will also be MK-30 drone targets, all of which will have enemy submarine target characteristics. All submarine contacts will be considered hostile and attacked including Illinois." He couldn't hold in a chuckle. "Like you might ever see her."

Carla gave Captain Prudsen a dirty look. "How are the MK-30 targets and Illinois augmented?"

Lieutenant Jim Meyer, the squadron weapons officer, responded. "The MK-30 targets I ordered are slightly noisier than current threats."

Captain Prudsen commented, "The Illinois and Pittsburgh are not augmented. Sometime during the exercise Pittsburgh and Illinois will be forced to have a close encounter with each other. That will be the true test."

Carla spoke up. "Given the Block III Illinois is the quietest submarine in the world and Pittsburgh is the oldest in the United States fleet, you are guaranteeing Pittsburgh gets sunk. This sucks just like the other crap we have to put up with."

Karen Young gave Carla a harsh look. "Weps, calm down. We asked for this." Her tone shifted to her Spock-like manner. "Captain Prudsen, a question related to procedural compliance. It is a major grading factor in a TRE. My question, given that all of our sonar and fire control publications and procedures are no longer maintained by the Navy, are we going to be evaluated poorly because we use cut and paste, internally generated documents for our operations?"

Jerry Prudsen smiled. "XO, the answer to your question is 'yes.' You asked for this and you will be evaluated as significantly below average in that area because of your lack of procedural documentation."

Karen gave Captain Prudsen the evil eye. "That hardly seems fair. We start out below average and work our way down from there."

Jerry smiled. "That's the way it is."

Drake, looking frustrated, stood, and looked at Karen. "XO! That's the way it is." He looked at Jerry. "Captain Prudsen, why don't you and I retire to my cabin and let your team and my team go over the TRE details?"

Captain Prudsen nodded and followed Drake out of the wardroom.

The chief of the boat leaned in between Karen and Carla in his best fatherly way. Mike Reinhart was the most respected COB in the Pacific Fleet. He had arrived right after Drake Chandler and had been a major player in Pittsburgh's ascendancy to the battle efficiency winner for the Pacific Submarine Fleet ever since.

"Ladies, it's best to back off a bit here. We asked for this, and even though they no doubt have stacked the deck against us, at least we have a fighting chance. Most in the squadron and the fleet know the full story."

Karen nodded, and Carla grimaced and spoke up. "You're right, COB, but you'd think they would give us a real chance. I'm just tired of always being the laughingstock and called 'that piece of shit' when I know we are better than any ship I've ever been on."

The COB nodded. "Weps, you weren't here for the glory period just before the new commodore arrived."

Karen looked at the TRE team and whispered, "Our ship and crew are the best in this damn squadron and probably the entire Pacific Fleet. They are planning to have us fail miserably." The COB nodded. "But at least we'll go down fighting."

Drake and Jerry Prudsen entered the CO's stateroom and sat at the desk. A CS brought coffee up for both men. Captain Prudsen was visibly upset.

"Chandler, you better get your bitches under control. Young and Kelly were way out of line down there. They piss me off."

Drake knew he had to calm Jerry Prudsen down, but he needed to defend his officers. "Captain, I think it's inappropriate of you to refer to my XO and weapons officer as 'bitches.' They're tough because they've fought the old-boy network their entire careers. And now, they feel you and Commodore Sails take every chance to hurt Pittsburgh."

"You mean, like you did to me when I was XO on the Maryland."

Drake looked Captain Prudsen directly in the eyes. "That, sir, was a major safety screw-up that you were personally responsible for. I just did my duty and stepped in to provide supervisory oversight while you and your captain and engineer were passed out drunk in a local strip club."

Captain Prudsen was spun up. "Don't give me that shit, Chandler. You were an asshole then and you're an asshole now. I'm not sure what I dislike worse: you or your split-tail crew members and especially your XO and Weps. God, I hate women

20

on submarines."

Drake shook his head. "Captain, that's not fair. Those two women are better than any XO or weapons officer in this squadron."

Jerry laughed. "Bullshit! Fair is whatever I say it is."

In ComSubRon Fifteen Quarters on USNS Frank Cable AS-40, the submarine repair ship assigned to Guam, Captain Stephan Sails, Commander Submarine Squadron Fifteen, sat in his office on the O-3 level, drinking coffee. He was looking at his message traffic. He'd assumed command four months ago and was beginning to think accepting this assignment was a mistake.

He was a Pentagon-D.C. sailor, extremely successful working his way around the five-sided Pentagon puzzle palace, the agencies and Congress. The admirals he worked for had opened many doors and he took advantage of everyone. When Sails was a junior officer and department head, his commanding officers had been rock stars in the submarine force. He got pulled along in their wakes as they rose in the Navy hierarchy, finally being assigned as the president's military aide. He and President Lincoln Jefferson had become close.

His shaky XO tour about did him in, until he was saved by his first commanding officer. His command tour had started out a disaster, but an old friend selected his ship for a series of high-profile submarine demonstration operations. The outcome of these operations was used to influence key members of Congress and heads of major agencies of the need for enhanced funding. This put Stephan in his element, and he pulled these off with spectacular success. Not having to operate in the demanding climate of everyday submarine operations, fight for tight resources and compete with his fellow commanding officers, allowed him to become the submarine force rock star.

Now he was in the western Pacific at the pointy end of the global war for peace, and everybody wanted his submarines: the same submarines he had helped President Jefferson successfully work to reduce in number to meet his budget priorities. Now it was biting him in the ass. Throughout the Pacific, admirals were pissed at him for not providing submarines for their needs. Christ, didn't they realize he was the premier submarine commodore and a personal friend of the president of the United States?

Over the ship's announcing system, he heard "Commander submarine force Pacific fleet arriving, commander submarine Group Seven arriving." What in the hell were Collar and Mains doing here?

Rear Admiral Mike Collar, ComSubPac, was Commodore Sails' immediate boss. Navy Captain Ralph Mains was the senior submarine captain in the Pacific theatre, the man who operated his submarines when they deployed. Both had been WestPac sailors their whole lives. They had no idea how the real Navy operated.

Stephan jumped up just as his chief yeoman, YNC Roberts, stepped in the door. "I'm on my way to meet them, sir." Bringing Roberts with him from D.C. to Guam had been a good move; he knew just what Sails needed and often well before he needed it.

Admiral Mike Collar loved going up the gangplank of the ComSubRon Fifteen flagship. Over a decade ago, he had held that position. Captain Ralph Mains similarly enjoyed being in Guam, the home of the real working submarines of the United States Navy. ComSubRon Fifteen and the Frank Cable were the lifeblood of submarine operations from the Northern Russian coast, past North Korea and China, all way through the Indian Ocean and the Persian Gulf. Their submarines and all the east coast submarines deploying to the Pacific and the Persian Gulf totally depended on the support of his squadron, and the repair and logistical support of the Frank Cable.

As they arrived on the quarterdeck, they saluted the American flag, then saluted the young lieutenant junior grade and requested permission to board. Chief Roberts stood behind the officer of the deck and saluted.

"Admiral and Commodore, we're surprised you are here. We didn't know you were coming."

Captain Mains gave him the evil eye. "That's interesting. Our visit request and travel itineraries were receipted by you four days ago."

Chief Roberts knew there was a problem in Squadron Ops that needed his attention. "Well, we're sorry, but we weren't expecting you."

Rear Admiral Collar and Captain Ralph Mains came into Stephan's office, led by YNC Roberts. Michael Collar was eight years senior to Stephan and had been ComSubPac for almost three years. Among the operational submarine forces, Michael Collar was their leader. Stephan's first CO, Vice Admiral Rentner, had just taken over as the commander, U.S. Submarine Forces in Norfolk, Virginia, and was the actual leader of the entire submarine force. Like Stephan, he was a D.C. admiral, and Rentner was looking forward to getting Rear Admiral Collar retired.

Ralph Mains was another at-sea operator. At sea almost all of his time in the Navy, he had been in command of USS Houston when it pulled off the spectacular capture and rendition of a major Al-Qaeda leader in Somalia. Subsequently, he was in command of USS Florida as it rained down Tomahawk cruise missile hell when the president ordered the U.S. participation in overthrowing

23

Muamar Gaddafi in Libya. Mains had also been ComSubRon Fifteen two commodores prior to Sails.

Stephan moved forward to shake hands. "Admiral, Commodore, I am surprised to see you. How were the flights?"

Admiral Collar shook his head, "Flights suck!" Captain Mains just nodded his head in agreement. "C-17s are better than the old C-141s and much better than a C-130, but – my God! – they all suck."

"Stephan, how are you liking your new job?" Admiral Collar asked. He knew Stephan was having trouble adjusting to the fast pace of operations in the western Pacific. Also, his past – when he had helped the Secretary of Defense cut the number of fast-attack submarines in commission in order to save money – was coming back to haunt him.

"I'm starting to get the hang of it."

"Great!" responded Admiral Collar. "But right now, let's get down to business. We've got a problem. As part of the president's new Peace in Our Time Initiative, the ballistic missile defense cruisers and destroyers have been pulled off the North Korean coast with no thought of who is going to maintain the Congressionally mandated electronic surveillance. We need to get a submarine in there to do that mission ASAP."

Ralph Mains just shook his head. "This president is so naive. All you must do is look at recent world history. But no one is going to persuade the president that his supposed personal charm has no effect on the likes of Kim Jong-un. The guy is crazy. The pulling out of our ballistic missile defense cruisers and destroyers is extremely dangerous. I don't care how much the Chinese have professed to control North Korea; this puts our country in extreme danger if Kim wants to launch a real nuclear missile. No one controls that madman."

Stephan was taken aback by Captain Mains' comments. "Captain, I think you are incorrect. The intelligence on North Korea's nuclear weapons capability and their ability to marry it with a ballistic missile is still uncertain. The president believes people are overstating the concern. Indeed, this agreement shows that Kim is seeking better relations with the West, not confrontation as in the past."

Ralph Mains shook his head. "Stephan, you've spent most of your time in the theoretical world of D.C. and the Pentagon. We out here in the Pacific are at the extreme pointy end of the spear and we go against bad guys on a daily basis. We look at things differently."

Captain Sails tried to respond, but Admiral Collar silenced him with a gesture. "Ralph, let's get directly to why we are here."

Ralph rotated in his chair to look at Stephan. "Stephan, as the admiral noted, we need to immediately get a submarine off the coast of North Korea to monitor communications and movements. But there is an even more dangerous crisis in the Persian Gulf with the Iranians having established a 'Persian Caliphate' and intending to close the Gulf. Their Ghadir bottom-hugging submarines make any operations in that environment suicide. We are very shortly going to need an exceptional submarine crew who can handle that very serious threat."

Admiral Collar spoke up, "With the cutbacks in defense spending and high temp submarine operations, it looks like the only two submarines available are Tom Witson's Illinois and Drake Chandler's Pittsburgh, both here in Guam. Right now, we need to solve our immediate problem off North Korea."

Ralph Mains followed up, "We want to make sure we send the right ship to the right mission."

Stephan Sails smiled. "Exactly! Tom Witson is my top CO

and the president's former aide. There is no decision. We send Illinois to the Gulf and that piece of shit Pittsburgh to North Korea."

Captain Mains shook his head in surprise. "Whoa! Not so fast, Stephan. Chandler and his crew are one of the best trained and most experienced crews in the fleet."

"That's not the way I see it. Pittsburgh's the oldest sub in the fleet with the most aggravating commanding officer I can think of. No one thinks Chandler and Pittsburgh belong at sea, let alone on a mission."

Admiral Collar looked surprised. Obviously, the issue with Drake Chandler exposing Stephan's father-in-law's complicity during the attempt to sabotage the submarine variant ABM system was still very much in his mind. There was more to the Sails-Chandler relationship he did not understand.

"I am not sure of your characterization of Drake Chandler or his crew. Drake and Pittsburgh have served us well in their role as a developmental weapons and sensor systems platform. Based on Drake's postgraduate thesis, he is considered the Navy's expert on submarine operations in the Persian Gulf."

Captain Mains rose. "Well, Admiral, we have a great opportunity to watch Pittsburgh as she goes one-on-one against Illinois. Stephan is conducting a TRE right now on the undersea test range."

Stephan looked at Admiral Collar. "I was pissed when Chandler went around me and asked for an at-sea TRE. We haven't run at-sea TREs since our funding was cut more than ten years ago."

"Actually," Collar said, "I made that call before you assumed your new command. My staff and I kept getting calls from Chandler bitching about the unfairness of Pittsburgh doing

26

TREs against other ship crews in the simulation trainers where his crew couldn't use their own one-of-a-kind systems. But as much as I like Drake Chandler and Pittsburgh, I have a special agenda. I need and expect Tom Witson to embarrass Pittsburgh during the TRE. I need political ammunition against Naval Reactors to decommission Pittsburgh once Drake completes the Persian Gulf mission. We just don't have the funding it takes to keep a one-of-a-kind 688 class Pittsburgh at sea."

Ralph Mains looked shocked at the admiral's remarks. He had not heard that before, although it made sense. "Well, then I suggest we go down to the UTRCC and watch the Illinois-Pittsburgh bloodbath."

Chapter 2

For such a fancy name, the Undersea Test Range Control Center, or UTRCC, was little more than a tired doublewide trailer in the support complex at the head of the Polaris Point pier. Inside, on the back wall, were two huge plasma screens: one showing the horizontal view of the range, sixty miles long by twenty-five miles wide. Directly below, the second screen showed the vertical water depth over the range from the surface to two thousand feet. Lieutenant Commander Ed Haley, the squadron operations officer, stood in front of a podium, shuffling papers. Shortly, he would be briefing his commodore, Admiral Collar, and Captain Mains.

Stephan Sails sat in his center chair, thinking about what Admiral Collar had said about Illinois embarrassing Pittsburgh, so he could get rid of the expensive-to-maintain old 688 class submarine. My God, that old piece of shit has sail planes.   He also saw his opportunity to nail Drake Chandler for what he did to his father-in-law, the former undersecretary of the Navy for research and development during the submarine ABM fiasco two years ago. The ABM system worked well on surface ships and getting it on a submarine provided greater flexibility and safety now that Chinese long-range anti-ship missile systems had become more sophisticated. The president thought having an ABM system on a submarine was destabilizing in the world of diplomacy. Stephan had worked with his father-in-law in Washington with the president and the agencies to get the program killed.

Chandler not only worked behind the scenes with Raytheon and Northrup Grumman to get the system operational, but in the process, uncovered falsified documents his father-in-law had sent to Congress about the poor performance of the missile. Chandler's unauthorized disclosure of those documents got his father-in-law fired and almost sent to prison. The president paid dearly in political capital as members of Congress pressed him for his failure to fund the program. Despite the media's efforts to hide this, it was all over the internet. The president eventually prevailed, and the program was shut down, but not before Drake Chandler and Pittsburgh successfully demonstrated the system.

His thoughts were interrupted by the arrival of Collar and Mains.

Stephan stood. "Admiral, welcome to the UTRCC. Let me introduce you to Ed Haley, my operations officer. He will be briefing the exercise." After the routine greetings, Admiral Collar and Captain Mains sat down next to Stephan.

On the display were submarine symbols for Illinois in the upper left-hand corner, moving from left to right. In the lower left-hand corner at the extreme edge of the range, Pittsburgh's symbol was also traveling left to right. Out ahead of Illinois was a bright MK-30 target drone symbol that had been sketching a jagged course from left to right. Pittsburgh did not appear to have a target, but in the lower left-hand corner a helicopter symbol moved onto the range immediately behind Pittsburgh.

Lieutenant Commander Haley started his brief, referring to the upper screen. "Admiral Collar and commodores, welcome. The exercise has been going about thirty minutes." Pointing to the symbol for Illinois, he continued. "Illinois picked up her target about twenty minutes ago at about 20,000 yards and is tracking and moving in to shoot." Indicating Pittsburgh's symbol, he said, "Pittsburgh is here, and her target will be dropping shortly."

Captain Mains chuckled. "What's the noise level of Illinois' target? Any brighter and you'll need to replace the plasma screen."

Haley looked around at the others, not knowing what to say. On the screen, a dim MK-30 target-drone symbol appeared about 1000 yards dead astern of Pittsburgh, moving directly at it. Collar and Sails smiled conspiratorially.

Ralph Mains was obviously irritated. "So much for fair play. There is no way Pittsburgh can keep that target outside 500 yards. And Jesus Christ, what noise level are you using on it? That bastard is quiet!"

LCDR Haley looked concerned. "Sir, this is exactly how Captain Prudsen set up the exercise and, yes, that target drone has the lowest acoustic signature available."

The control room on Pittsburgh was packed with crew and TRE evaluators. Crew members were all on sound power telephones or wireless headsets.

Drake Chandler stood in his normal stoic pose – arms crossed with his left hand on his chin – between the fire control panel and the geographic plot just in front of the conn. The room was quiet and orderly, although it was crowded with evaluators and with sailors manning plots and panels. Drake's eyes moved quickly among all parties, and he smiled – this is now we train. Karen Young, the fire control coordinator, stood next to Drake, looking at the fire control sonar display. Carla Kelly was just right of Karen in front of the weapons control panel. The COB, as diving officer of the watch, was in front of the ship's control panel. LCDR Frosty Allen, the ship's engineer, had the deck and was on the conn looking at the sonar display.

Karen nodded her head and tapped the shoulder of Lieutenant Chris Pott on the fire control panel as he adjusted his solution. "Captain, Master One bearing 271 is classified target drone with enemy submarine characteristics. Our solution puts

Master One on the west of the range at 23,800 yards, course 355, speed 8. I don't think that is our target."

Drake walked over to the geographic plot, then looked at the sonar display. "I agree. That's Illinois' target and it's fucking loud."

Karen coolly looked at Drake. "It's been in the water for fifteen minutes and eighteen seconds. In accordance with doctrine, Illinois will close into a firing location to demonstrate minimizing counter fire."

Drake shook his head and chuckled. "XO, you are a walking Tactical Development Manual encyclopedia." He leaned forward. "But, XO, something's not right. They have both of us on the extreme southern end of the range and we are tucked into the southeast corner with little maneuvering room."

Karen nodded, "Yes, sir."

Captain Prudsen stood behind Drake, trying to see around him. Drake made it as difficult as possible and turned to look at Captain Prudsen. "Captain, you put my ship in a very difficult position to start the TRE. We have no room to the edge of the range on the right."

Prudsen smiled. "Sounds like you have a tactical problem."

Drake shook his head, looked at Karen and pointed to the sonar display. "XO, have sonar shift our display to the towed array endfire, and make sure they're looking for a helicopter."

Karen nodded. "Yes, sir."

As Drake and Karen watched the display, a dim trace appeared in the endfire beam of the array. As Karen listened to a new communication from Sonar, Drake moved toward the ship's control party. "Ahead Standard, right full rudder."

Karen looks surprised. "Captain, Sonar reports a helo

directly behind us. They are picking up its blade rate and it sounds close."

Drake looked at the sonar display. "On the helm, continue right, steer 060. XO, those bastards are going to drop our target right on our ass. Make sure Sonar looks at our starboard baffle."

Captain Prudsen looked at the plot and smiled. In a haughty tone, he addressed Drake. "Captain, may I remind you? You are not allowed to exit the range."

Drake ignored Captain Prudsen. Karen spoke, "Captain, Sonar picked up a broadband trace Master Two bearing 190."

Drake calmly said, "XO, set range 1000 yards, course north."

Karen looked stunned and opened her mouth to speak.

Frustrated, Drake snapped, "Now, goddam it!" In a cold, professional tone, he ordered, "Snapshot Master Two, Tube Two!"

Karen watched Lt. Pott update his counsel. "Solution ready."

Carla observed her fire controlman enter inputs to the torpedo, and reported, "Weapons ready with the exception of minimum enable."

In the background, the officer of the deck called out, "Ship ready!"

Drake resumed his arms-crossed, chin in left hand pose. The atmosphere in the attack center was surprisingly calm. Drake had repeatedly exercised his crew on such scenarios and his training had paid off.

Karen looked at Drake, "Sir, range 750 yards and entering our starboard baffle."

Drake looked the ship's heading; it was swinging nicely, coming up on 060. "On the helm, ease your rudder to right five steady course 120." He turned to Karen. "Range rate?"

"Fifty yards per minute, opening and increasing."

"Very well. On the helm, continue to course 250."

Despite the very close encounter, things were still quiet. Drake addressed the attack party.

"Attention, attack party. An enemy submarine drone was picked up directly behind us at about 1000 yards. We have moved out to the east to let it pass astern and keep it outside 500 yards. I intend to steady on a southwesterly course, let the target open to minimum weapons range and shoot it with one MK-48 ADCAP torpedo. Carry on."

The attack center party listened, nodded, and went back to their duties.

Jerry Prudsen smiled like the Cheshire cat as he came up behind Drake. He had been waiting for this ever since he set himself up as the senior officer on board for the exercise. "Well, Chandler, looks like you got counter detected."

Drake gave him a hateful stare. "Wrong, Captain. If the target had got within 500 yards, the UTRCC would have turned the drone at us and increased its speed."

Jerry knew Drake was right, but he was still pissed, and started to say something, but was interrupted by Karen.

"Target will be at minimum weapons range in thirty seconds."

Drake gave Prudsen a dismissive look. "Very well." He looked at the geo plot, then at Karen and Carla.

Carla nodded. "Captain, target at minimum enable."

Drake nudged Prudsen out of the way. "Very well. Shoot!"

Petty Officer Smith, at the firing panel, pushed the tube Two fire button. There were three loud noises as the torpedo ejection pump went through its cycle: Thuk! Thak! Shhhhhhhhh!

Along the Pittsburgh's port side, a torpedo shot out of the upper torpedo tube, sank, then the engine started up and the torpedo accelerated forward and turned in front of Pittsburgh.

In Control, Carla checked her indication. "Weapon engine start, running normal coming to the pre-enable course. Weapon will enable in ninety seconds."

Drake walked over to the geo plot. The track of their target was engulfed by the search cone of the torpedo. He looked at the top of the plot, where the Illinois' target Master One's track was in the path of their weapon. He leaned forward and pointed to the plot coordinator, Lieutenant Tom Dawson. "Lieutenant, show me a point 2000 yards directly ahead of Master One and be ready to calculate a torpedo correction to that point."

Pings could be heard over the sonar speaker: ping...ping...ping....

Carla announced, "Weapons enabled."

Karen verified, "Sonar holds the weapon enabled."

The weapons control panel operator excitedly called out, "Detect! Detect! Acquired!"

In the water behind the target drone, Pittsburgh's torpedo was actively pinging. It increased speed and the pings come at shorter and shorter intervals as the torpedo closed the drone. When the torpedo was close to the target, it turned away to prevent damage to the drone target. It dove, changed course, and stopped pinging. A successful hit!

In the attack center, the pings on the sonar speaker ceased as Carla called out, "Turnaway!" Karen quickly reported that Sonar had verified turnaway. Pittsburgh had hit its first target.

Drake leaned next to Captain Prudsen and smiled. "Well, your little gambit didn't work too well. Outside 500 yards and a hit."

Prudsen walked away, disgust plain on his face.

Drake called over to Lieutenant Dawson on the geo plot, "Plot, what's my torpedo correction?"

Dawson had already calculated it, and reported, "Left sixty degrees, sir."

Drake acknowledged and looked at Carla. "Weps, pre-enable the weapon, change transit depth to shallow, set speed low and insert a left sixty-degree course change."

Petty Officer Smith made the torpedo adjustments on his panel and Carla reported, "Weapon pre-enabled, slow speed, transit depth shallow and left sixty-degree course change inserted."

Drake moved to the center of the control room and announced, "In Control, shift primary contact of interest to Master One. Fire control, send best solution to plot." Quietly, the Pittsburgh attack party shifted contacts of interest.

Chapter 3

Pittsburgh's torpedo had gone under the target drone, come shallow, and changed to a course to the left so that it would intercept Master One.

Drake pulled Karen and Carla to the plot. "XO, as you noted, I think Illinois is closing her target to get in the optimum firing position. That would be about here." He pointed to a position on the plot about 6,000 yards astern of Master One's track. "That means she will be there in the next ten minutes. WEPS, I want this torpedo transit at shallow depth and low speed. I want to enable a torpedo right here, so Illinois has something to think about."

Karen smiled and in her best Spock-like manner, said, "Yes, sir. Recommend going to firing point procedure on contact Master Three. I'll generate the target."

Drake nodded. "Firing point procedure Master Three, tube Four. The XO will set the solution."

Karen directed Pott to put a contact in at range 13,000 yards on a bearing of 273 with a speed of zero knots. When it was entered, she gave the standard report. "Solution ready, Master Three."

Carla followed with, "Weapons ready."

The officer of the deck reported, "Ship ready."

Drake took one last look at the geo plot. "Shoot."

Petty Officer Smith pushed the tube Four fire button. Again, the torpedo ejection pump went through its thuk-thak-shhhhhh cycle. Outside the Pittsburgh's port side, a torpedo shot out of the lower torpedo tube. It sank, the engine started, it accelerated forward and turned in front of Pittsburgh.

While Drake resumed his arms-crossed pose, Jerry

Prudsen stood in the middle of the controlled activity, totally unable to comprehend what Chandler was doing. Jerry had lost control.

In the Illinois attack center, handsome Tom Witson, commanding officer, stood in the middle of two rows of panels. He was looking forward to his one-on-one with Drake Chandler later in the evaluation. He intended to kick Drake's ass. Tom had come to Squadron Fifteen from duty as the vice-CNO's aide and was the commanding officer of the newest and most capable fast attack in the world. He was frustrated that, other than Commodore Sails and Captain Prudsen, the lower level squadron staffers and enlisted personnel didn't recognize him as the best commanding office in the squadron. They all considered Chandler to be the CO who walked on water. Fucking Chandler had never been to D.C. and had no idea how the submarine force operated in the real world. Well, the new commodore and his Chief Staff Officer Jerry Prudsen certainly knew who the top dog was.

Tom knew he was on the quietest and most capable submarine in the world. He had a good crew and wardroom, except for Executive Officer Roger Gatlin. Gatlin had spent all of his at-sea time on boomers and, on top of that, he was a nuclear power officer candidate – not Naval Academy. He didn't fit in, and how he'd made it to XO, Tom didn't know.

The Illinois' control room and attack center were much better laid out than was USS Pittsburgh's. New optical technology periscopes had eliminated the need to have the control room on the upper level. As a result, the control room and attack center were on the much wider middle level. With this larger space, the sonar workstations and operators could be collocated with the fire control and weapons workstations. That could be a blessing or a curse.

On Illinois it was a curse. Chaos reigned in the attack center. Although they'd picked up their MK-30 target twenty minutes earlier, if it hadn't been for the target's loud noise level, the disorder in the attack center would have prevented them from locking up the solution. In this case, the fire control algorithm had solved the target motion analysis with little operator interaction.

Roger Gatlin was the fire control coordinator. Despite his many efforts and training sessions, he could not get the different panel operators and supervisors to listen to him or develop any form of discipline. The captain consistently undermined his efforts to establish a level of professional calm. The panels operators and supervisors rarely listened and often talked over one another. There was a lack of coordination. Chaos. Roger had tried to get the squadron deputy commander to address the problem with his captain, but he was afraid of Tom Witson and would do nothing.

Tom Witson couldn't understand why they didn't have a firing solution on the target. "XO, what the fuck are you doing? I'm ready to shoot."

Roger countered, "Captain, the solution is ready, but doctrine says we should close to minimize opportunities for counter torpedo fire."

Tom Witson shook his head in exasperation. "I ask you again, XO, are you ready to shoot?"

Subdued, Roger said, "Solution ready."

There was an interruption, as the sonar coordinator called out, "Hold very weak transients bearing 077. Appears to be a distant torpedo firing."

Tom Witson chuckled and announced to his team, "Well, fucking Chandler and his split tails got their first shot off. We're going to kick their ass in about six hours."

The crew laughed obligingly.

Tom addressed his XO. "OK, boomer boy, we'll close the target to minimize counter fire." He turned toward the pilot station. "Ahead full."

Frustrated, Roger Gatlin argued, "Sir, I recommend we close at a slower speed to maintain contact and sonar search capability. We will lose them at that speed."

Tom Witson was pissed. This was the opportunity he had been hoping for, and he wasn't about to let Gatlin blow it for him. "Okay, XO, that's it! Get the fuck out of here. You're fired!" He looked at his engineer, LCDR Mike Malone. "Eng, take over as fire control coordinator."

Lieutenant Commander Roger Gatlin grudgingly took off his head phones and handed them to Malone.

On the Pittsburgh, Captain Prudsen moved in behind Drake. "Just what the fuck do you think you're doing? I want you to shut down those weapons! This is crazy."

Drake uncrossed his arms and turned to look at Prudsen. "There is still a second enemy submarine target drone and the USS Illinois out there. I intend to attack them with my torpedoes as prescribed in your orders. Do you have a problem with that?"

Jerry Prudsen really hated the way Chandler flung his TRE directive in his face. "Chandler, you are such an asshole. Just what do you think you are going to accomplish? There is no way those exercise weapons can reach any target, and you fired a million-dollar torpedo at nothing. You are just going to make it easier for me to fail you."

Drake looked at the geo plot, did a mental calculation and turned back to Prudsen. "Then, Captain, at least please stay out of the way and let me fail!"

From the plot, Lt. Dawson called out, "Captain, the first weapon is 2000 yards ahead of Master One's track!"

Drake pulled Karen over to the geo plot. The first torpedo was definitely out in front of Master One. The second torpedo was about 4,000 yards from its aim point.

Karen nodded. "I like it."

Drake looked over to the weapon panel. "Weps, insert a left eighty-degree steer and enable the first weapon."

"Left eighty degrees. Aye." Carla tapped Petty Officer Smith, and he inserted the steer and enabled the weapon. "Captain, left eighty-degree steer inserted into the first weapon. First weapon enabled."

Drake and Karen watch the plotters adjust the torpedo's path. It was going right at Master One, Illinois' target drone.

Drake smiled. "Weps, enable the second weapon."

Carla and Smith both executed the order,

"Captain, second weapon enabled."

Karen smiled as she listened. "Sonar holds both weapons enabled." On the sonar speaker, active torpedo pings could be heard.

Drake had placed his first weapon, very close to fuel exhaustion, right on Master One's track. Smith called excitedly, "First weapon. Detect! Detect! Acquired!"

Petty Officer Smith looked concerned. "Lost the wire. Seven per cent fuel remaining."

Drake moved between Karen and Carla. "This may get real exciting, depending on where Illinois is."

The first torpedo was now at slow speed, actively searching, with no control from Pittsburgh. Suddenly, it dove, turned left, increased speed and started pinging. When it steadied on course, it was pinging and directly in front of the underwater target drone. The torpedo acquired the target, and the pings came at shorter and shorter intervals as the torpedo closed the drone. The torpedo achieved turnaway, diving, changing course, as it had on the first target drone. As it went under the target and slowed, the USS Illinois was seen directly in front of the torpedo. The torpedo leveled off, recommenced pinging, and turned toward the Illinois.

On Illinois' starboard side, the second torpedo slowed and started pinging. It was 4,000 yards away.

Tom Witson waited in his most professional stance behind the Illinois' pilot station to watch the attack center. The attack center was still noisy, but a sense of their commanding officer's invincibility flowed from the operators.

Tom looked at his geo plot. "All ahead two thirds, right five-degree rudder, steady course 120. Contact should bear about 355. Firing point procedures on the target tube One."

The fire control coordinator and other panel operators updated their solutions. The sonar coordinator was feeling pretty good. As the ship slowed, two new traces showed up on the screens in addition to their primary contact. The new traces both had indications of torpedoes. One directly north on the expected bearing to the target and one dead ahead as the ship turned through 090. Then the sound of active torpedo pings dominated the noise in the attack center. He shouted, "Two torpedoes in the water! One bearing 357, one bearing 088."

In accordance with torpedo evasion procedures, the officer of the deck ordered an increase in speed and rudder to left full.

Tom Witson was shocked to see two torpedoes coming at the Illinois. He grabbed his officer of the deck and shook him. "Bullshit! Stop! Do not take evasive action. There's no way a

41

torpedo can be out there!'"

The OOD announced, "Ahead two-thirds. Stop all torpedo evasion."

Tom Witson froze as he stared at the sonar displays with a shocked expression of disbelief. Over the control sonar speakers, he could hear tightly spaced pings become almost steady tones. Ping…ping…ping…ping…ping-ping-pingpingping ....

The sonar supervisor saw and reported, "Sir, both torpedoes are locked on and range gating on us. Both are inside 1,000 yards."

Drake and Karen huddled together at Pittsburgh's geo plot.

"If Illinois is where we think it is," Drake commented, "things will get exciting very soon."

Petty Officer Smith called out, "Second weapon, detect, detect, detect, acquired." Lt. Dawson updated the plot and Lt. Pott updated his solution at the fire control panel.

Captain Prudsen pushed his way in to look at the geo plot. He immediately saw the second torpedo had acquired Illinois. Just then, a very excited sonar supervisor reported out over the MC, "The first weapon has acquired and locked on to target bearing 258."

Drake looked at Prudsen. "Well, Captain, sometimes the best laid plans of mice and men go astray."

Jerry Prudsen turned in disgust to say, "Fuck you, Chandler."

The locked-on torpedo on Illinois' starboard beam increased speed and closed. When it got close, it achieved turnaway and changed depth and course so as to not hit Illinois.

The locked-on torpedo directly ahead of Illinois was

closing at a high rate of speed. At 1000 yards, the torpedo engine, out of fuel, stalled. Its pinging and propulsion ended, but the 4000-pound, now buoyant torpedo was still moving at over fifty miles per hour. It continued to close Illinois. The torpedo collided on the aft vertical stabilizer and disintegrated, leaving the stabilizer damaged. The noise from the collision reverberated throughout the weapons range.

Everyone in the Pittsburgh attack center heard a loud noise on the sonar speakers. Drake and Karen looked at one another. Carla came to stand between Drake and Karen.

"What was that?" Carla asked.

Drake looked at the sonar display. "Our second weapon is still running like a normal turnaway. Something happened with the first weapon."

In the UTRCC, tension was high. The plasma displays showed Illinois caught between Pittsburgh's torpedoes. The second torpedo fired by Pittsburgh was in acquisition on the starboard side of Illinois and had just gone to turnaway, demonstrating a hit. Somehow, the first torpedo still had fuel remaining. It had already demonstrated kills on both drone targets and was in acquisition directly ahead of Illinois and closing fast. Suddenly, its audio showed sounds of its engine slowing, then stopping, and its tracking pinger stopped transmitting. In the next moment, a loud collision was heard on the range speakers.

Admiral Collar and Commodore Sails looked shocked. Captain Rains just smiled and shook his head.

Collar chuckled. "What the hell just happened? How did Chandler get those exercise weapons all the way over to Illinois?"

Captain Mains stood up and stretched. "Admiral, looks

like your boy Witson and his brand-new Block IV Virginia submarine just got his ass handed to him by a 35-year-old 688."

Stephan Sails was irate. "What the fuck was Chandler thinking about? He just destroyed a million-dollar exercise torpedo! And more than likely, we will have to dry dock Illinois to check for damage. Someone needs to be held accountable."

Mains moved to the rack of printouts. "Stephan, I think you are missing the point of what we just saw. Chandler and his crew are very good at submarining and understand how to fight their ship. We very often forget that technology is not everything when you fight in the underwater environment. It comes down to leadership, experience, training, and tactical savvy."

Stephan was no less infuriated. "I'm going to court martial Chandler for this stunt."

Collar sat shaking his head and smiling. "Stephan, I think you need to think about the persons who set up this exercise, and that includes you."

As Admiral Collar and Commodores Smiles and Rains departed, LCDR Haley picked up the range announcing system. "This is the range director. All submarines come to safety course north. When steady on course, immediately surface your ships. Range control certifies there are no contacts in the vicinity of either submarine. It is safe to surface. Once on the surface, submarines remain on course north at four knots. Directions for return to port will be forthcoming."

PART TWO – MISSION PREPARATIONS
Chapter 4

As Drake Chandler sat on the back of the bridge, his Pittsburgh entered Apra Harbor. It was beautiful sunny day, after all it was Guam, where "America's day begins." Pittsburgh followed Illinois into port, only to be delayed by Captain Prudsen demanding he be returned by a fast boat or RHIB.

When Captain Prudsen departed he was concerned, and fear showed in his eyes. He had set up this exercise and somehow a million-dollar MK-48 exercise torpedo was destroyed and there was a real possibility of damage to Illinois. He had refused to debrief Drake or even talk to him. He had ordered a boat to take him off the Pittsburgh immediately and it was obvious he was trouble.

Captain Prudsen's personnel transfer took about twenty minutes, but it had been a hilarious event. Although it was calm, the gentle waves still caused the RHIB to rise and fall alongside Pittsburgh. Captain Prudsen's impatience led him to mistime his step into the alongside RHIB. Instead of jumping on the rise of the RHIB, he stepped off when it was falling away. This resulted in him missing the side of the RHIB and falling face first into the boat, with his arms holding onto the RHIB and his legs dangling in the water between the Pittsburgh and the boat. It was all anyone could do to keep from laughing.

When Drake was Submarine Squadron 19 squadron engineer, he had conducted many "Leaps for Life" in the Strait of Juan de Fuca. They were scary, but you either leaped or you spent the next three months on some submarine's ballistic missile patrol or mission.

Pittsburgh was delayed because Tom Witson attempted to do a no tug assisted landing with Illinois and got turned bow-into-the-pier until the tugs came alongside and moved him into position. Drake smiled as he remembered standing next to Captain Mains many years ago watching as an SSN tried to do the same thing. Drake never forget his words.

"You know Drake, there are no points for smart ship handling on nuclear submarines, but there are lots of demerits."

In the cockpit, Drake watched Carla Kelly oversee young Lieutenant Junior Grade Chis Pott as he maneuvered Pittsburgh between Orote Point and the Glass Breakwater. Chris was a NUPOC, or Nuclear Power Officer Candidate. Chris had no pretentions about his background; only a desire to do a good job. He was smart, articulate and a breath of fresh air. He quickly surpassed the Naval Academy and NROTC junior officers on board and was the XO's favorite JO.

As they approached the entrance to Polaris Point, two Navy tugs were just slowing, getting ready to take them into the pier. A submarine, with its single propeller or a propulsor behind the rudder, had little control as its 8,000-ton bulk moved into a pier or alongside another ship. With the ships control surfaces being in front of the rudder, a submarine has little control at low speeds. Loss of control could cause serious damage to the submarine, a pier or other shipping.

At the piers, the Tender Frank Cable was Med-moored at its usual location. On the pier there were high levels of activity with supply carts moving parts, and golf carts moving sailors, contractors and supervisors. Illinois had returned to port first and was tied up to the pier bow-in. Pittsburgh waited for the submarine camels -- special floating structures that safely separate the deep underwater submarine hulls from the pier or, in this case, another submarine -- to get in place before it would tie up parallel and outboard of Illinois.

Drake loved the new Z-drive-type marine propulsion unit tugs that had come to Guam. One could come alongside with the heavy fenders keeping them from hitting Pittsburgh's hull. He had taught his officers that he liked the tugs tight alongside with a breast line to his number 3 cleat just after the sail, and spring lines to his number 2 cleat just forward of the sail, and his number 4 cleat back by the after-escape hatch. Tied like this, the tug's Z-line 360 thruster had full control of the ship.

Young Lieutenant Pott watched Carla handle the pilot, then work with the tugs to smoothly put Pittsburgh next to Illinois.

Once the ship was safely tied up, Drake met with the COB and XO in his stateroom. The COB had made the rounds of all the shops on the piers and Tender and Karen had been up to Squadron OPS.

Drake inquisitively asked, "Any news?"

The COB spoke first. "Lots of buzz going around the shops about how we kicked Illinois' ass, but there is real caution and fear about how the Commodore is going to react. He was not happy."

Karen spoke up. "That's similar to what I got at Squadron, but they are carefully tip-toeing around. I cornered the OPS Officer Ed Haley in his office and shut the door. He told me something's up. He said Admiral Collar and the Commodore had some harsh words in the Commodore's cabin, but he didn't know the result."

The COB responded. "That sort of lines up with the scuttlebutt I heard in the tender goat locker. It seems that the commodore doesn't fear or respect the admiral even though he is ComSubPac. He knows something and, evidently, he doesn't feel

Admiral Collar can do anything to him."

Drake nodded. "I'm not surprised. The commodore and Admiral Renter the new ComSubForces are pretty tight."

Just before departing the ship, Captain Prudsen had called and informed Drake that, at the commodore's direction, he was initiating an Article 15 investigation into his failure to follow orders during the TRE, resulting in the destruction of a one-million-dollar exercise torpedo and his summary court martial would be the next day.

It was early afternoon, but Drake knew he had to get legal help. Knowing the Submarine Squadron JAG lawyers would be of no help, Drake called and met with the ComNavMarianas JAG XO, Lieutenant Colonel Sally Ann Field, United States Marine Corps. Sally, or "Harm," as her friends called her, had been in Drake's company back at the Naval Academy.

On graduation she had become an F-18 fighter pilot and had distinguished herself in Iraq and Afghanistan. On her last tour, she was attacked by a group of Iranian fighter aircraft. She and her wingman got three of them before the others hightailed it for home. By a freak accident, a piece of a destroyed aircraft hit on the cockpit and got sucked into one of her engines. The damaged piece went through the thin fuselage and cut deeply into her left leg. Severely injured, she maneuvered her plane back toward her carrier, but the damage had been too great, and she'd punched out and parachuted into less-than-friendly territory.

After holding off two bands of Taliban marauders for over six hours, she was finally rescued by a search-and-rescue helicopter. She was flown immediately to Ramstein Air Force Base in Germany, where she had survived twenty hours of surgery with the loss of her left leg below the knee and severe scarring over much of her body.

She was presented the Navy Cross by the president, but her flying career was over. She was given her choice of assignments and she chose to go to Georgetown Law School and become a Navy JAG officer.

Harm was shocked when Drake told her what was happening. She told Drake to not worry about it; she would investigate and get back to him.

Harm was unable to get Captain Prudsen's investigative report. The Submarine Squadron 15 legal officer had been obviously upset when she called him. He claimed he had no idea about some commodore's Summary Court Martial. Finally, she got hold of Commodore Sails' yeoman. He reluctantly provided her a document of charges, but it was not an official copy.

Even so, after reading it, she was confident that nothing would come of it. There was no proof of any violation of the UCMJ. It was all conjecture, and the senior officer present afloat or TRE team leader should have been charged – not Drake Chandler. She called Drake and told him what she had learned and said she would meet him on the submarine tender the next day.

The next morning, Drake was in his stateroom putting on his summer white uniform, frequently checking himself in the mirror. There was a knock on the door and Carla Kelly entered. Drake didn't want anyone to know what was happening about the Mast.

Carla gave Drake an admiring once-over and smiled. "My, what are we getting dressed up for?" She teasingly smirked, "Let me guess. A celebration party for the victor?"

Drake frowned. "Don't I wish. What do you need?"

"We've completed all preparations for weapons handling. Request permission to load war shot torpedoes."

Drake couldn't hold in a smile. Carla was Drake's favorite

department head. Not only smart and dedicated, she had an air about her that exuded confidence, and she had brought her department and divisions together in a tight-knit group. She often got under the XO's skin, but at the end of the day, Carla was the go-to lieutenant that Karen and the COB relied on.

He replied "WEPS, load war shot torpedoes."

As Carla prepared to leave, she turned back with questioning concern in her eyes. "We really kicked Illinois' ass, didn't we?"

Drake gave her a look over his glasses. "Why do you ask?"

Carla responded "Well, I know Captain Prudsen was pissed, but then he is sort of a jerk. But I heard some scuttlebutt that the commodore is also unhappy."

Drake straightened and thought about what he was going to say. "Yes, we kicked Illinois' ass, but kicking ass and doing well are not necessarily the same thing."

Carla was irritated. "How could that be? We did everything right and more."

Drake gave her his fatherly look. "Weps, it's complicated, and in this case being right may not turn out well." Drake had to fight back a tear of anger. "Weps, make sure your weapons teams know they performed well. I am proud not only of them but of the whole crew."

Carla gave him a look of disbelief and turned to leave.

Drake spoke up. "By the way, please let the XO know I am going to the supply cages and then going to the tender."

Carla looked confused. "What's up?"

Drake gave her a glance. "Again, Weps, nothing that concerns you."

Carla left, and Drake finished getting his uniform in its

best condition. What was this Mast going to be like? He had done nothing wrong except that he had been disrespectful towards Jerry Prudsen, a toad if there ever was one – an officer whose weaknesses had been demonstrated in inspections and activities where Drake had been a key participant. He was weak and vindictive, but he had powerful friends. Drake checked the mirror one more time. With everything looking good, he departed.

Chapter 5

Topside, TMI Randy Pender had his weapons handling team working smoothly. He had never enjoyed his job the way he did on Pittsburgh. He knew this was the result of working under Captain Chandler and Lieutenant Kelly.

Looking over at the Illinois he saw his friend and old TM C-school classmate, Butch Anderson, doing the same thing with his team. Randy noted Butch had no women on his team.

He knew how get in a good dig. "Hey, Butch, it's a lot easier getting torpedoes off your sub through the torpedo tubes."

Illinois had not fired either of its two exercise torpedoes and they had to offload them before they could reload with war shots. Anderson gave Pender the finger. "Fuck you, Pender. You were lucky."

Pender laughed and called out, "Oh, is that what you call it? Luck. I just thought someone who got his ass kicked might be more humble."

Carla came up out of the midships hatch and moved forward of the sail, observing the banter. "Pender, knock it off. You stay focused on what you're doing."

Pender knew he had been caught and gave Carla his best puppy dog, I-got-caught look. "Yes, ma'am."

Carla continued forward, inspecting the torpedo skid and lines that had been laid out.

With Carla right beside him, Pender turned and asked the same question she had asked Drake earlier. "We really kicked ass, didn't we, Lieutenant?"

Carla realized that Pender had heard the same rumors she had, so she addressed the group in a voice loud enough that the

Illinois torpedoman could hear. "Guys, we had a great day in the TRE and, yes, we did very well against an exceptionally good opponent. Now, let us stay professional and get those war shots safely down below and stowed."

Just then, Karen came out of the hatch and heard Carla's pronouncement. She saw the Illinois' torpedomen and could tell they were not happy. She moved toward Carla. "Weps, let's get going."

Carla looked up and started walking toward Karen. "Yes, ma'am."

As they walked aft, Karen asked, "What did the captain tell you?"

Carla stepped up on the brow. "He really looked depressed and just told me to tell you he was heading to the supply cages, then he had things to do on the tender."

Karen nodded. "Hmm, in trop whites, no less."

Carla nodded. "Yup."

They reached the brow to Illinois, saluted, rendered honors to their topside watch, and moved across to the Illinois. Approaching the Illinois topside watch, Karen said, "Permission to cross."

The Illinois topside watch had seen them coming and had a scowl on his face. He said nothing. Karen repeated, "Permission to cross."

The topside watch gave a weak salute, mumbling, "Cross."

Karen and Carla rendered honors to the topside watch and the American flag and headed for the pier.

The topside watch mumbled under his breath, "Fucking split-tail bitches," as he gave them the finger.

Karen looked down the pier at the group of people huddled around the area of Illinois' rudder. She and Carla turned that way and walked toward the group. Looking out at Illinois, they saw the serious dent in the top of her rudder.

Carla started to laugh, saying, "Wow! Our torpedo really smacked 'em."

Karen looked closely and in her academic manner, commented, "The exercise torpedo safety feature no doubt failed on the first torpedo we shot."

Tom Witson, dressed in summer white, had watched Karen and Carla walk toward the group huddled by the rudder. The irritation and bile in his stomach churned and the sight of these two inflamed him even more. His reputation and possibly upcoming mission were at risk and these two Drake Chandler pawns were no doubt part of that.

As Tom approached Karen and Carla, they saluted. "Good morning Captain Witson, I'm Karen Young, the XO –"

Before she could finish, in a burst of anger, Tom condescendingly shot back, "I know who you are. You two must think you're pretty smart."

Carla, never one to take rude behavior well, stepped forward with a mischievous smile. "Well, sir, I'm the weapons officer whose two exercise torpedoes kicked that submarine's ass. Is that ship yours?"

This comment caught Tom Witson and his ego off guard, and he moved toward Carla. "You insubordinate bitch."

Karen stepped in between them and gave Carla a harsh look. "Knock it off, Weps."

Tom stepped back, realizing he was treading on thin ice with two female officers. "What you did was a violation of tactical weapons protocols and you just got lucky."

Karen gave Captain Witson her best Spock-like demeanor. "Well, sir, not exactly. We had eliminated our target and had been tracking your target at twenty-two thousand four hundred and thirteen yards."

Tom broke in. "That's bullshit."

"No, sir, that is the truth. Captain Chandler successfully directed our first weapon to your target, then directed me to place a second torpedo six thousand yards behind the target and enable it."

Beaming with delight, Carla pointed to the damaged rudder and with her best southern drawl retorted, "It was purrrrty easy pickings."

Karen gave Carla a harsh look. "Captain Witson, I apologize for Lieutenant Kelly's comment. It was inappropriate."

Tom didn't hear Karen's apology. "I know all about you two, and none of it good."

At that moment, in the background, the tender announcing system was heard. "All quiet in officer's country while commodore's Mast is in progress."

A diabolical smile came across Tom's face. "I've got to go, but when your boss gets his ass kicked today, I'll make sure you know the meaning of appropriate."

Carla looked at Karen with concern.

Chapter 6

The commodore's cabin had an eerie atmosphere, having been broken down and set up for a judicial hearing. Commodore Sails, the convening authority, and Jerry Prudsen talked on the far side of a long table covered in a green felt cloth. Lieutenant Colonel Sally Ann Field was looking over a copy of the charges. The ComSubRon 15 JAG Lieutenant, who, according to Sally, knew nothing about the Mast, was behind them getting papers in order. Captain Mains stood by the room entrance quietly watching.

When Drake entered, he looked around and saw Harm, who looked upset. Drake moved to her. "What's up?"

Harm disgustedly said, "The copy of the charges given to me yesterday is not what is being used today. They have more charges added."

In sparking whites that looked like they just came from the tailor, the handsome and slick Commander Tom Witson entered the room like the Crown Prince meeting his peers. He immediately went to Stephan and Jerry. "Commodore, so good to see you. Jerry, good to see you, too."

Stephan beamingly shook his hand. "Same here."

Tom, knowing he had control, pumped his hand. "In all the last-minute activity since I arrived and your change of command, I never got a chance to tell you that Admiral Rentner sent his congratulations and wanted me to give you his best wishes. Oh, and I was with the president about a month ago in Hawaii and he also wanted to pass on greetings to you."

While Stephan Sails' face lit up, Captain Mains', Harm's, and Drake's showed disgust.

The CSS-15 JAG lieutenant came forward and interrupted Stephan. "Sir, you wanted to make sure we got started on time."

Stephan acknowledged, "Yes, yes. Thank you." He then composed himself into a harsher, more formal posture. "Tom, thank you for all that, but we need to proceed." Looking over at Drake, he continued, "Commander Chandler, please approach the table and join Captain Witson."

The atmosphere tensed. Drake and Captain Mains noted that Commodore Sails referred to Drake as a commander and Tom Witson as captain. Drake and Harm both approached the table.

Stephan looked up and was surprised to see a Marine Corps lieutenant colonel beside Drake. "I'm sorry, but who in the hell are you?"

Harm came to attention. "Sir, I am Lieutenant Colonel Sally Howes, U.S. Marine Corps and JAG Corps, currently serving as XO ComNavMarianas, JAG Office. Let me say, I feel your last comment about my client's rank was disrespectful and inappropriate considering the environment we are in." Harm pulled a small recording device out of her pocket and placed it on the table. "Commodore, if you apologize, I will delete that comment from my court record."

Stephan knew he had been out of line and he wasn't ready for this. "I'm sorry, but you are not welcome at my summary courts martial, and you may leave."

Harm gave him a snarky smile. "In what section of the Uniform Code of Military Justice does it allow a convening authority to deny a defendant the right to counsel? You might want to have your JAG lieutenant look that up."

Stephan gave a haughty look, but Harm came right back at him. "On second thought, since I experienced how your young lieutenant failed to understand his duties under the UCMJ by lying to me last night, I will save you the time: The UCMJ doesn't allow you to do that."

Stephan regrouped and, realizing he couldn't win on the legal issues, he tried another tactic. "Lieutenant Colonel Field, I respect the JAG Corps and your position, but this is an informal summary court-martial proceeding. No doubt you have a great legal mind, but you know nothing of the warfighting, tactical, operational and command issues I am confronting in dealing with Commander Chandler."

Harm relaxed out of her attention statue, moved closer to Stephan, and looked him right in the eye. "Sir, I'm not happy with the way this is proceeding. I am not sure you understand the pile of shit you are getting yourself into."

Stephan tried to say something, but Harm raised her hand with authority.

"Commodore, right now I have the floor and you can respond when I am finished."

Stephan realized that, with a recording device running, he had to be cautious.

Harm continued. "First, my client, in this case Captain Chandler, commanding officer of USS Pittsburgh, and I have not been treated with the respect and deference we deserve in a legal proceeding like this. I have respectfully referred to you as 'commodore,' not 'Navy captain,' yet you refer to Captain Chandler as 'commander' and to me as 'lieutenant colonel' when 'colonel' is the normal term for my rank. Second, I am a United States Marine Corps officer with broad experience in all aspects of warfare and will be able to understand and support my client as needed."

Stephan thought he saw his opportunity to embarrass this obnoxious JAG bitch and get her out of his court martial. "No, Colonel, you don't. I will be addressing issues related to life and death in wartime. I don't care how many books you have read or where your JAG desk has been located. You cannot fathom wartime operations to be a part of this proceeding. You need to leave now and take your recorder with you."

Captain Mains had been watching Harm in amazement. She was spectacular. He also saw the blue-and-white ribbon with a bronze V at the top of her four-row cluster. He spoke up. "Colonel Field, I see you have a blue-and-white ribbon with a combat V at the top of your cluster. Could you tell us what that is and how you got it?"

Stephan spoke. "Captain Mains, this is nonsense."

Ralph responded. "I think we should listen."

Harm looked down at her ribbon with trepidation and then looked at Drake.

Drake spoke up. "Commodore, Colonel Field can't speak to that without emotion. She and I are classmates and longtime friends. That ribbon is the Navy Cross with the combat V. She was an F-18 fighter pilot on her fourth deployment to the Persian Gulf. She and her wingman were attacked by six Iranian fighter aircraft. They got three of them before the others hightailed it for home. By a freak accident, a piece of a destroyed aircraft hit her aircraft just below the cockpit, got sucked into both engines and severely damaged her left leg. She was able to maneuver back toward her carrier, the Vinson, until the damage was too great and she had to punch out and parachute into less-than-friendly territory. After holding off two bands of Taliban marauders for over six hours, she was finally rescued by a search-and-rescue helicopter. She was flown immediately to Ramstein Air Force Base in Germany, where, after twenty hours of surgery she survived, but with the loss of her left leg below the knee and severe scarring over much of her body."

Ralph moved over and put his arm on Harm's shoulder

and shook her hand. He looked back over at Stephan. "Commodore, this Marine Cops JAG officer has more wartime and tactical operational experience that any submarine officer going back to Whitey Mack, Freddie Warder, Mush Morton and Dick O'Kane. She brings insight into whatever you think you are trying to do today."

Stefan realized that he had lost the battle, and started his obligatory grovel. "Colonel, I apologize for denigrating your experience without knowing the entire story. You may certainly stay."

Stephan's apology infuriated Harm. As she moved back to her position next to Drake, she commented, "My experience and background have no relevance in protecting the rights of any sailor or marine accused of a crime. Commodores and commanding officers have huge latitude and discretion in executing justice in proceedings like these and as prescribed in the UCMJ. They must go above and beyond any reproach in protecting those whom they have charged with crimes or infractions. May I suggest we proceed?"

Stephan fought off a desire to go across the table and strangle the smug lawyer. My God, he worked for and was a close friend of the president of the United States. What she didn't know, was that he fully expected to get appealed to ComSubPac, but by the time that appeal got there, Admiral Collar would be gone and one of Admiral Renter's friends would be there to uphold the conviction and punishment.

Stephan picked up his script and addressed Drake. "Captain Chandler, having reviewed the USS Illinois – USS Pittsburgh Tactical Readiness Evaluation and the Board of Inquiry investigation, I find that commanding officer USS Pittsburgh used poor judgement in not following the directions of Captain

Prudsen, the senior officer onboard, to command shutdown of his exercise weapons." He looked directly at Drake. "My God, that was a direct order from a senior officer."

Drake sternly looked straight ahead until Harm nudged him and whispered, "This is where you tell your story."

Drake got control of himself. "Sir, Captain Prudsen never ordered a command shutdown of any weapon, as the recording of the evolution I made will show. He only asked me what I thought I was doing. I reminded him his Tactical Readiness Evaluation War Orders were to sink and destroy all enemy underwater vessels that were to be assumed enemies. He then told me I was an asshole and there is no way that exercise weapons could reach that Illinois target drone. He said I was just going to make it easier for him to fail me." In a condescending voice Drake concluded, "I was 'fighting' my ship, sir!"

Jerry Prudsen started to fidget and look around for a hole to hide in. Stephan was surprised that Drake had tried to defend himself, but then he had seen Colonel Field nudge him. He realized he needed to dig himself out of the hole he'd dug. Stephan asked, "Did you not know Illinois was over on the west side of the range?"

Drake gave him a look of incredulity. Again, Harm nudged him. "Well, yes! It was a TRE! We were both on the range with safety depth separation."

Stephan shook his head in disbelief. "Then why did you proceed?"

Drake was not sure about his next step, but he threw caution to the wind. "Tactically, two things came into my mind: I had an excellent solution on a very loud second enemy submarine target drone to the west that I was sure was for Captain Witson and the Illinois; my target had been dropped right on top of me, letting me use minimum fuel for my attack. I knew by slowing and taking the exercise weapon to a shallow transit, I could get it close to the other target drone and possibly successful engage it."

With a look of sarcasm, he turned to Captain Prudsen. "You know, demonstrating superior submarine skills! It was, after all, a tactical readiness evaluation. As for Illinois, Commander Witson, he's a big boy in command of the Navy's most advanced submarine."

Commodore Sails, sensing victory, gave Drake a hard look. "So, you intentionally put a weapon in the vicinity of another submarine causing millions of dollars of damage."

Drake was taken aback. "I beg your pardon, Commodore, but I was in a fight for the life of my ship. I did what I was trained to do and that was to successfully engage and kill the enemy. I was not Commander Witson's babysitter."

Chaos broke out at the table as Captain Sails, Captain Prudsen and Tom Witson turned on Drake and all spoke at once.

Harm spoke up. "Commodore, you are falsely accusing Captain Chandler of intentionally causing damage to the Illinois. That was not in the charge sheet your lieutenant provided me or my client."

Captain Sails looked offended, but Harm continued. "Sir, you do realize the next stage of the evaluation was a one-on-one torpedo engagement where both ships would be firing weapons at each other. I may only be a Marine Corps JAG officer, but I know submarines fire exercise torpedoes at each other. Captain Chandler had no idea his exercise weapon would collide with Illinois and not turn away."

Stephan saw he was losing control and he raised a hand. "Colonel Field, thank you for that, but I have heard enough. We need to move on."

He turned his attention to Tom Witson. "Captain Thomas Witson, I and the Board of Inquiry find that commanding officer USS Illinois used poor tactical judgement in approaching a potential target at high speed such that the ship was unable to process potential threats resulting in his ship being hit by a stray exercise torpedo. Do you have anything to say for yourself?"

Tom Witson, having been briefed in advance, sucked it in. "No, sir."

With this part of the Mast going as planned, Captain Sails moved to the punishment phase. "Captain Witson, you will be given a non-punitive letter of reprimand, and it is hoped that this will help you improve your future performance in your profoundly serious role as commander of a nuclear-powered submarine. You are dismissed."

Tom Witson saluted, did an about face and smartly departed with a smile on his face. This had gone just as he and the commodore had planned it. A non-punitive letter was a nothing burger that just gets thrown away.

As he left, Stephan focused on Drake. "Captain Chandler, I and the Board of Inquiry find that commanding officer USS Pittsburgh disregarded the safety protocols resulting in major damage to U.S. Navy assets."

As this point Harm broke in. "What, you are not going to let the accused have a chance to defend himself? Did you not understand anything I said earlier? This is not in accordance with the UCMJ. You are violating Captain Chandler's rights."

Stephan now raised his hand with authority. "Colonel Field, I am commander submarine Squadron Fifteen. I don't report to ComNavMarianas, as you do. I am a commodore and I have been provided all the facts needed in this case by my staff. I don't need some JAG lawyer telling me how to do my job."

Harm and Drake were shocked. Harm spoke up. "You know this will be overturned on appeal."

Stepan arrogantly grinned. "You have your chain of command, I have mine." He turned his attention to Drake. "Commander Chandler, you will be given a punitive letter of reprimand, and it is hoped that this will help you improve your future performance. You are dismissed."

Drake, Harm and Captain Mains were shocked at the disparity of punishment. Captain Mains moved next to Harm and Drake, and nudged them to leave. Drake and Harm saluted, did an about face and departed.

Captain Mains turned to Stephan. "Stephan, your punishment was way out of line. I feel you let what happened to your father-in-law cloud your judgement."

Stephan was ready for this. "Ralph, you are not his commander and not accountable for his actions. He has shown me nothing but insubordination in the few weeks I have known him. I intend to have him relieved of command as soon as I can."

As Drake and Harm departed the commodore's cabin, Tom Witson was waiting for him in the outer office. He stepped out and intercepted them. He was surprised and upset to see Harm with him. He obnoxiously sneered, "Excuse me, Ms. Field, but I have something I need to discuss with Chandler."

Harm was shocked at his impudence. "My, how rude and unprofessional you golden boys get when someone steps on your parade. No problem, Mr. Witson. I need to get back and prepare an appeal."

Harm looked at Drake. "I'm still invited to your Persian Gulf Operation brief tomorrow."

Drake was still smiling from Harm's encounter with Tom Witson. "Yes, yes, 1000 in the conference room on the third level.

My XO Karen Young has you on the invite list."

Harm looked at Tom. "Now, you two boys play nice."

Tom Witson had been irritated before his interaction with Colonel Field. Now he was livid. "Chandler, everybody in your chain of command hates your fucking guts and you just damaged my ship. You're an arrogant asshole and I am going to make sure you lose your command."

Drake still shocked by his punitive letter. "Well, Tom, it seems to me, because of your tactical stupidity, you actually came out on top. First, you get a slap on the wrist and I get a death sentence."

Tom Witson moved in and forced Drake against a bulkhead. "Chandler, I've spent more time backing down fast attacks during special operations than you have at sea."

Drake smiled and looked him in the eye. "Oh, yeah, that certainly showed during the TRE."

Tom took a swing at Drake, but Drake caught his arm and pushed him aside. Frustrated, Tom Witson yelled out, "Fuck you and your fucking split-tail crew!"

As Tom Witson stomped out of the room, he collided with Commodore Sails, who was passing by. Stephan looked into the office and back at Tom. "Are you okay?"

Tom extracted himself from the collision. "Yes, sir. I'm just peachy."

As Tom walked off, Stephan entered the office. He gave Drake a harsh look. "Chandler, that stunt you just pulled is going to be the end of your career. You're not smarter than the Navy and you're certainly not smarter than me. I'll see to it that you never go anywhere."

Drake, still smarting from his interaction with Tom Witson, recognized he was on thin ice, but he had to respond to the verbal threat from his boss. "Commodore, I always do what I think is best for the Navy and my country. The major difference between you and me is that I don't weigh the political bullshit before I do the right thing, and I don't use my power to settle personal scores."

Chapter 7

The previous day had been bad for Drake, but now he had a chance to restore some confidence and demonstrate his expertise. He was going to brief ComSubPac Admiral Collar and all the senior submarine officers and commanding officers in the Pacific about operating submarines in the shallow Persian Gulf. Admiral Collar had left three days earlier, so he and most of the attendees would be coming in by video conference.

Drake Chandler was one of the Navy's most knowledgeable officers on submarine operations in this area of the world. This had been his focus during his short one-year tour at the Navy's post graduate school before taking over command of Pittsburgh. As he, Karen and Carla busied themselves with preparations, the various members of the audience entered. The squadron operation's conference room was set up as a theatre. Captains Mains and Prudsen, Tom Witson and his XO Roger Gatlin, and several other officers were in attendance.

Harm walked in and came up to Drake. "This better be good, Chandler. I left my boss a bit pissed when I told him where I was going."

Karen shook Harm's hand. "So, you're Captain Chandler's classmate. He talks about you all the time. So good to finally meet you."

Harm smiled. "Well, Drake speaks very highly of you."

Carla had just come from the electronics room behind the podium, and on seeing Harm she rushed over. "Oh, my God! It's Colonel Sally Field." Carla put out her hand and shook Harm's hand excitedly. "You were the greatest speaker we ever had at the Naval Academy. Every woman midshipman wanted to be just like you, me included."

Drake laughed. "Okay, Weps. Then how in the hell did you end up here instead of some foxhole?"

Harm shook her head. "Carla Kelly, right? I remember you. Our Marine Corps spies and recruiters at the Academy were trying to get you away from the clutches of the damn nukes."

Drake spoke up. "And thank God, they didn't."

Everyone was waiting for Commodore Sails. Admiral Collar finally came up on the video conference. "Captain Chandler, let us get started. You can brief Commodore Sails later."

Drake started. "Admiral, commodores, and fellow submariners, thank you for taking the time to listen to a summary of my post-graduate thesis on operating submarines in the Persian Gulf."

Karen brought up a slide of the Persian Gulf. "The Persian Gulf. Even with the expansion of our country's oil reserves, the region is still the largest source of oil for the world. The gulf is small and shallow – the deepest part being about three hundred feet. Its high salinity, strong currents and high noise levels make it a blessing and a curse for a submarine attempting to seek out and find targets, but make it easy for it to hide. The Iranians have seven diesel electric attack submarines, mostly of Russian design, and twenty-seven mini submarines, the most lethal being the 23 Ghadir class. The Ghadir is designed to lie on the bottom waiting for a target to get close. They are normally deployed close to the coastline where it is relatively quiet."

Commodore Sails, frustrated, entered and announced to the room. "We need to end this presentation. I just got off the phone with Admiral Rentner, the submarine force commander. As we heard earlier, we need to get a submarine off the coast of

North Korea. As much as the admiral fought it, things got moved up. The president has already pulled our ballistic missile defense cruisers and destroyers off the North Korean coast. Congress is demanding he carry out the national directive to maintain electronic surveillance. We have to send a sub in there now."

Stephan turned to Drake. "Captain Chandler, I'm sorry, but we will have to do this later."

Captain Mains smirked. "Here we go again with unintended consequences of the president's naïve foreign policy."

Stephan spoke up in defense of his president. "Captain Mains, I was part of the early negotiations for the president's initiative. I can assure you there is total sincerity and thoughtful research into those discussions."

Captain Mains shook his head. "Yeah, yeah, yeah, I'm sure there are, but that doesn't mean they aren't naive."

The room had broken into several conversations as the tender repair officer, Commander Tom Marshall, entered. He walked up to Commodore Sails. "Commodore, I've got bad news. The divers just finished up on Illinois' aft vertical stabilizer. The damage from the exercise weapon is such that she needs to be dry-docked for repair. Probably the best we can do is to get her into drydock and out in about four weeks."

Stephan looked perplexed. "Tom, thank you."

The repair officer left and everyone around the table started looking at Drake and Tom Witson. Drake, Karen, and Carla looked extremely glum.

Commodore Sails looked at Admiral Collar on screen. "Admiral, with respect to what sub we send, this settles it. We'll have Pittsburgh ready to go in two days."

Admiral Collar looked at Drake. "Captain Chandler, unfortunate for us, but you're the only submarine available for the

North Korean mission. It's not my first choice, but it looks like Illinois will be the only sub available to carry out the Persian Gulf mission when she gets out of drydock."

He then looked at Captain Mains. "Ralph, how about riding Pittsburgh up to Yokosuka, where, I assume, they will pick up their spook team?"

Ralph answered "Roger that, sir. Always looking for submarine ride time and I've been wanting to see Chandler's interesting mixed-gender SSN crew."

Drake knew Commodore Mains was kidding – he spent days at sea on different submarines. Drake was disappointed but rallied. "You're in luck. The rider's bunk is the XO's stateroom."

Karen gave him an odd look but then smiled. "Yes sir, my upper bunk is perfect for a rider."

Chapter 8

It was a beautiful spring day in Washington D.C. The cherry blossoms had fallen but the good rains and warm days had made Washington a bright green carpet studded with beautiful white structures.

Susan Grains was in her office, fuming. Congress was threatening action if the president didn't get their mandated real-time electronic surveillance of the Korean coastline in place. For the last fifteen years, this had been done by the Navy's Anti-Ballistic Missile Defense ships. Now that she had gotten them removed, the Navy was putting a goddamn submarine off the North Korean coast to do the surveillance mission.

She had just got off the phone with her friend and former tryst Commodore Stephan Sails. He had been the president's aide and the son-in-law of a very influential party donor. He was as handsome as they came, and, wow, was he good in the sack. He was aware of her concern and as much as he had tried to stop it, he was about to send a submarine with some out-of-control submarine commander on the surveillance mission. Evidently, he had just been court martialed, or something like that, for violating the rules of some exercise. Just what she needed – a wing nut out there trying to make a name for himself.

Susan needed to get the president's staff on board to stop this submarine snooping on the North Koreans. She was confident she could browbeat the president's chief of staff, Clark James, Secretary of Defense Tom Reynolds, and Secretary of the Navy Judith Wilson, into pulling this sub off the coast of North Korea. James and Reynolds were simple-minded men who could be led around by a hot pussy in a tight skirt and some cleavage with the proper hints that made their dicks quiver. She had that page in her play book and she was ready to make that move. She also felt she could handle Judith Wilson.

Michelle Pak, Susan's assistant, knocked and entered the room. Michelle had been a doctoral student of hers at Harvard. She was the daughter of South Korean parents who emigrated to the United States with their families in the late 1970s. Michelle was the most resourceful of any of her staff, especially when it came to issues related to Asia and especially the Koreas.

Susan had run into some issues getting her a security clearance, but if Secretary of State Hillary Clinton could put a non-secure server in her home, she had known she could address this. Susan had pulled the director of the Defense Counterintelligence and Security Agency aside and resolved that.

Michelle had a set of papers and talking points for her. She said, "Doctor Grains, the group has gathered. They are not in a good mood."

As Susan rose from her desk, she said, "Fuck 'em."

Susan entered the conference room with a frown, and with a flourish slammed the door behind her for maximum effect. Clark James, Tom Reynolds and SecNav Judith Wilson, were seated. She walked to the head of the table and sat. "Well, ladies and gentlemen, what have you done to screw up the president's initiative today?" She looked at Tom. "And you, Mr. Secretary of Defense, tell me again why we're sending a submarine off the coast of North Korea?"

Tom Reynolds had become use to this behavior from the president's NSA. He had succumbed to her sexual play before, but now he held his ground. "Susan, the president's Quadrennial Defense Review identifies monitoring of electronic transmissions from North Korea as a priority mission. This is the formal document that we use as the basis for funding for the armed services. Senators and congressmen don't take lightly to presidents ignoring a document like this."

Susan looked right at him. "Okay, but this could impact our new relationship with the North Koreans. It's the most important diplomatic initiative in many years. We need to get the Navy to back off."

Clark James could hardly control himself, but he knew Susan had significant pull with the president and not all of it because of her immense intellect and persuasive manner. He was quite sure the president was having some of her when his wife was away. "Susan, that's a bad idea. We have bad blood with Congress and the working levels of the Pentagon and if that got out, we'd have lots of trouble. They're already upset."

Susan gave a disgusted laugh. "When I was back at Harvard, our faculty and my people really understood what was important in diplomatic dealings with other states." Susan stood and walked behind them. "Listen closely. Anything that might impact the president's North Korean initiative has to be eliminated and we don't need some goddamn submarine driver screwing up the efforts."

Michelle entered, came up to Susan and whispered in her ear. "Doctor Grains, I have Mr. Song from North Korea on secure line one."

Susan nodded and looked at the group. "I need to take this call. This meeting is done. Let's meet again tomorrow and let's see if you can grow some cojones and get that submarine out of there."

As everyone left, Michelle moved to a secure phone on the table and punched three buttons. Susan sat down next to the phone and took the handset from Michelle.

Susan's demeanor immediately changed. "Mr. Song, so good to hear from you. Thank you for returning my call."

"What can I do for you Susan?"

Susan continued "Mr. Song, I am sorry, but we have a situation … well, a *requirement* I was not aware of for monitoring transmissions and communications off your coast."

Jong Song knew exactly what this was about. Michelle had fully briefed him only yesterday. He just smiled. "Surely you no longer are concerned about our intentions. Why can't the president just not follow that requirement? After all, he is your commander in chief."

Susan looked frustrated. "Don't I wish! But, unfortunately, it's politically more complicated than that. He can't make that move. But maybe you can assist in helping me to convince our government to remove this submarine from your coast."

Jong Song was surprised at how well he had gained Susan Grains' trust. He was aware that few in her Congress and Pentagon trusted her, and he certainly didn't trust her either. But she had the total confidence of the president. He also knew she was a darling of the American media. He replied, "Certainly. How can I help?"

Susan was relieved. "I was just told we are sending in a submarine, the USS Pittsburgh, in the next two days, to conduct that surveillance of your coast. I would consider it a favor if you might see to it that this USS Pittsburgh is roughed up a bit as it arrives. Something that I can use to get the Navy to possibly recall the submarine."

With the withdrawal of the U.S. Navy's BMD surface ships, Song was not surprised at this, but how lucky to have the president's NSA asking for this type of help. Now he not only knew who was coming, but the time frame he had to get ready.

"Madam National Security Advisor to the President, we thank you for trusting us and we will carry out your request."

"Thank you."

Then Mr. Song followed up. "Oh, and on a separate note, will you be traveling with the president to the San Francisco fundraising visit? Our consulate official, Mr. Po, will be there and he very much would like to meet you."

Susan smiled. "No. Unfortunately. I am stuck here in D.C. But at least, it's over the Fourth of July holiday."

Song acknowledged, "Well, I will inform Mr. Po. He will be sad. And Susan, I hope to see you in the near future."

Susan was happy she had been able to talk with Mr. Song. They had developed a great relationship and she trusted he understood the needs of international diplomacy.

As Susan departed, Michelle came over and shut down the secure telephone. She went to her office, picked up a satellite phone, left the White House and made a call.

Chapter 9

Getting Pittsburgh ready to go in two days was a huge endeavor. Stores, fuels, and parts needed to be loaded. Critical preventive maintenance that had been planned for later had to be rushed to get done. In addition, they lost a half a day breasting away from the pier to let Illinois be dead-stick transported to the port side of the tender for special preparations before she could be dead-sticked out to the floating dry-dock in the harbor.

Both ships had started their diesel electric generators and reduced electric consumption, so they could unhook the large shore-power cables that provided power to the ships when their reactors were shut down in port. One tug came bow into Pittsburgh and put over lines tied up to cleats just forward to the sail, and one back by the after hatch. Backing, the tug easily moved Pittsburgh away from the side of the Illinois. Another tug moved alongside of Illinois, pulled her away from the pier and transported her to the port side of the tender. Pittsburgh's tug easily pushed her back against the submarine camels alongside the pier.

Once shore power was reinstalled and the diesel was shut down, the stores started coming down the pier. Pallet after pallet of frozen, canned, and dry stores piled up on the pier. This was an all-hands-on-deck operation. The COB had a team of ship's chief petty officers working the teams of men and women as they first removed all stores from their cardboard boxes. They understood that cardboard is a serious problem on any ship. Cockroaches and other pests lay eggs in the cardboard and when it is stored, they can hatch, and the sub has an infestation.

Culinary Specialist Senior Chief Roger Smith was expertly

directing movement of the food down the hatch in a well-orchestrated choreography. When Drake assumed command, he told Smith that he had strong feelings about food service, having lived through a disaster as executive officer. He had lost his chief, and a crusty old CS first class petty officer took over. He immediately lost control of their food inventory and for the next six months, Drake had the worst experience of his Navy career. Drake had become an expert on food service, so the first time he met Chief Smith after assuming command he was on the offensive. The COB and Chief Smith were old shipmates and were ready once they calmed Drake down. They assured him he would never have problems with his CSs or food service. That prophecy had come true. Pittsburgh had won the Supply Battle Efficiency 'E' during the next three years, and for the last two years was the Ney Award winner for food service excellence in small messes afloat.

Smith knew that loading food into a submarine is all about the cycle menu. You only have one six-foot by ten-foot freezer to feed 120 men and women for up to six months. You have to eat your way through the freezer and the cycle menu tells you how to pack it back to front.

Before Drake got on board, the lowest rated men in each division were assigned to the cycle menu review team. Drake had known this wouldn't work, so he had directed that only the highest rated men in each division could be on the cycle menu team and he personally attended the team meetings. That had quickly set the tone for the importance of what they were doing.

The food came down as single cans and frozen items in a chain that went from boxes on the pier, across the gangway to the mid-ships hatch, down the hatch and then to the appropriate store room or freezer. There had never been enough room for all the food on a fast attack since the fleet boats of World War II. The excess food went onto the decks in the berthing spaces, so that personnel in the lower bunks had to make holes for themselves in order to get into their bunks.

Drake, Karen and Carla were heading up the starboard side of the tender to squadron when they met Commodore Sails and Jerry Prudsen walking aft. As they got near, they saluted. Drake said, "Good afternoon, Commodore, Captain Prudsen."

Stephan gave Carla a lustful look. She was one beauty and dressed in the working uniform that didn't do her justice. He could envision her in a bathing suit or, even better, something less. Stephan responded "Good afternoon, Captain Chandler. I don't think I ever got a chance to meet Kelly."

Drake was in no mood for small talk and objected to the look his commodore had given Carla. "Sir, that would be Lieutenant Kelly and she is my weapons officer."

Stephan recognized he was treading on less than safe ground and shifted his gaze to Karen. "Commander Young, I see my detailing you as liaison to Raytheon Missile Division served you well."

Karen still seethed at how the submarine force had screwed her by sending her to Raytheon and now she learned this Navy captain, her commodore, had done it. "If you mean your efforts to sidetrack my career by dumping me out-of-sight, out-of-mind, well, I think you failed. Captain Chandler pulled me out of there early to become his XO. Something that no doubt pissed on your no-women-in-submarines strategy."

Jerry Prudsen stepped forward. "Young, you're out of line. This is your commodore, and you need to show respect."

Drake stepped in. "Captain, again, that would be 'Lieutenant Commander' or 'Commander Young' to you, and I think the commander has a right to express her feelings to Captain Sails for his detailing efforts." Drake realized this was not going well as he looked at both men. "I beg your leave. We have work to do in preparation for our upcoming mission."

They all saluted and moved forward on the tender's main deck.

Stephan and Jerry remained behind, watching them. Jerry had not calmed down from the meeting. "Chandler is such an asshole, and his goddamn mixed-gender SSN is not good for the service. Boomers, okay. SSGNs, maybe. But fucking women don't belong on fast attacks."

Stephan turned his gaze to the harbor. "Totally agree, and the bastard intentionally disregarded Admiral Rentner's guidance on women. He convinced the NavPers Women in the Navy group that he could staff and run a mixed-gender 688 class SSN well before formal guidance came up from the Navy. So, he goes out and cherry picks his female officers and sailors."

Jerry nodded. "How in the hell did Chandler ever get command?"

"That's easy. When he was squadron engineer back in Bangor, Washington, he saved the shipyard commander's and the USS Wyoming's asses during a major propulsion plant disaster that could have brought the entire shipyard to its knees. Naval Reactors never forgot and, until now, you couldn't detail or touch Chandler without getting NR's permission first."

Jerry nodded. "Yeah, I remember. I was in his squadron as an XO. He got my CO relieved for cause and he almost got me. His holier-than-thou attitude really pisses me off."

Stephan put on a devilish smile. "Well, he pisses lots of people off but, Jerry, you did fuck up pretty badly."

Jerry blushed and looked down. "Okay, but his self-righteousness in handling the incident was uncalled for. After all, he was just a staff officer."

Stephan looked out over the harbor. "Trust me, Admiral Rentner wants him frog-walked out with his dick between his legs after the submarine ABM fiasco. Jesus Christ, he just should have left well enough alone. He found about the secretary's attempt to stop the system development and he went behind everyone's back and made it work."

Jerry chimed in. "Is that when your father-in-law got fired."

Stephan nodded. "Yeah, he was the sacrificial lamb. My wife was distraught and still harbors bad feelings. So, until now, no one's been able to touch him. But now, I've got him."

Jerry piped up, "But aren't you worried about Collar and Mains? They're sort of mentors to Chandler."

Stephen gave a snarky smile. "Yeah, they're a problem, but they will both be going away soon. Rentner is taking care of that."

Jerry looked up the main deck, seeing Drake, Karen, and Carla. "What's the story with Young? God, I dislike her. Evidently the two of you have a history."

Stephan chuckled. "I don't think she knew I was her detailer, but Karen Young was the engineer who uncovered the SSGN decommissioning fiasco and got several flag officers fired."

Jerry threw his hands up. "Let me guess. Naval Reactors loves her too."

"Yup! Naval Reactors protects her, too. So, when I got the chance, I detailed her as liaison to Raytheon's Missile Division and that should have destroyed her career. Then fucking Chandler plays the Women-in-the-Navy card and got her out and makes her his XO."

The sun was getting lower in the western sky, and Stephan and Jerry moved down the main deck and departed.

Forward on the tender main deck, Drake, Karen, and Carla stopped to look at the Pittsburgh next to the pier. Karen looked over at Drake. "Well, Captain, what was that all about?"

Drake gave her a resentful look. "That was the voice of those who believe style and appearance are more important than results. Those two were hot runners as JOs because they had connections and commanding officers and took care of them. Captain Prudsen didn't have the juice of Commodore Sails. He was married to the daughter of a fat-cat rising civilian in the DOD."

Carla, never one to think before she reacted, blurted, "So, Captain, what happened with you?"

Drake, knowing Carla's inquisitive nature, responded, "Nothing you need to know or will ever find out." He straightened. "But more seriously, you two get up to Squadron Ops and make arrangements to get our extra mission materials. I'll meet you back on board."

As Karen and Carla walked away, Drake leaned on the railing, looking out into the harbor. Flashes of his past came to his mind. He was a junior officer on USS Indianapolis in Pearl Harbor Naval Shipyard. He was in the wardroom, where his commanding officer was being chewed out by the shipyard commander. He could still remember his words.

"Jesus Christ, John, what the fuck do you think you were doing taking that fuel cell out without a joint test group on site?"

He distinctly remembered his CO throwing him under the bus. "Captain, it is not my fault. Lieutenant Chandler was following the procedure. He was directly at fault for allowing that fuel cell to be removed without the JTG."

Drake saw his XO and engineer nod their heads in concurrence, but the shipyard commander would have none of it. "Bullshit, Abbott. A fucking lieutenant junior grade should not have been in charge of that operation without senior officer oversight. Right now, I am relieving you of command with my chief of staff and I want a formal change of command done by next Saturday."

His CO had the audacity to ask, "Sir, am I being relieved for cause?"

The shipyard commander had disgustedly got up and started leaving. "No, but I should. You are almost at the end of your normal tour, so I just want to get you out of here as fast as possible." He had then looked at Drake's XO and engineer. "You two better start looking for some new lines of work."

That was Drake Chandler's first ship, and the stigma of working for John Abbot was with him to this day. No matter what he did, everyone remembered that incident. No one realized that he accomplished the difficult task with no problems and ahead of schedule. No, he was the JO who got his commanding officer fired. No one cared about him. He didn't have a mentor in high places taking care of him.

Drake looked up. A small tear had formed in his left eye. He loved this job. He was one of the best, but he had enemies.

Chapter 10

Two thousand miles north of Guam, a group of North Korean
senior military and civilian staff were meeting at the highly secret
Tonghae Satellite Launching Ground. Jong Song-taek looked out
the wide window onto the hectic activity among the many
launching site buildings and platforms. Summer was coming, and
the leaves were just starting to return to the few trees on the site.

He was the son of a peasant farmer whose father and
grandfather had fought in the Fatherland Liberation War in the
1950s. Jong had risen to power through crafty relationship
building and a cruel demeanor that made it easy for him to
eliminate his competition. He was smart enough to befriend the
young Kim Il Un as a boy.

Kim's ego made him easy to sway, but Jong had to
continually remind himself that he could turn on you at any
minute. Jong's father and grandfather had both died of starvation,
but he, the son and grandson, had learned how to work the system.
He had risen to the position of North Korean prime minister of the
cabinet.

Jong had been the key negotiator with the Americans in
their naive and narcissistic efforts to get North Korea to give up
their nuclear weapons. Their president was so easy. His perception
that everyone loved him and hung on his every word was so
obvious.

The president had never participated in a hard-nosed
negotiation in his life. Jong loved it when the president played his
patented American bigotry card. Jong had deftly feigned concern
when he had demanded some inconsequential point be included in
the agreement.

He had to work a bit harder on National Security Advisor Susan Grains. A good-looking woman who would stop at nothing to get what she wanted, she had the president's total confidence, despite that she too had never been involved in real-world international diplomacy, other than giving presentations at academic conferences.

He had played her well, and now she had total confidence in him. Being a harsh-looking, powerful man, women liked his company, and she was no different. In addition, she was an excellent sexual partner. My, what wonderful benefits came with this job.

Jong's staff was in a celebratory mood. They were all short-sighted men and understood little outside of their areas of expertise. But then, that was the way he had set it up. Men with vision and big aspirations eventually became threats.

Major No Kom-Sak was the first to come forward with a smirk on his face. An expert at missile telemetry, he had just started working with the Military Weapons Sales Directorate. He had proven to be adapt at this new task. "Congratulations, Mr. Song, on getting the 'Peace in Our Time Initiative' negotiated." He broke into in a laugh. "My, my, how Americans love their television sound bites."

Kim Shin-Jo, Jong's operation manager broke in. "The American president is so starved for a diplomatic legacy that he will believe anything that aligns with his ideology."

As everyone in the room laughed, Jong raised a hand in caution. "Let us be careful in our current euphoria. Our supreme leader has done well with the American president, but the American military can be dangerous."

All nodded. Kim beamed with euphoria. "Prime Minister, you played the Iranian card so well. I can't believe President

Jefferson gave us huge sums of money in cash along with releasing the sanctions that almost shut our missile program down. Just like the Iranians, they let us continue missile development and testing, and they even pulled their ballistic missile defense warships off our coast."

General Yun Lyun, the leader of the directorate for military weapons sales, spoke up. "When the supreme leader strikes out at the American paper tiger, our missile and weapons sales will explode."

All laughed. Major Kom-Sak looked at Jong. "But the part that is best is that the Americans will not be able to retaliate."

This was also the part that Jong loved the best. If the United States attempted a non-nuclear response, it would result in millions of South Koreans in the Seoul area being killed by the thousands of artillery pieces ready to fire on the border. They can't use their current nuclear weapons because all of the U.S. weapons are monstrous and would end up destroying both Koreas and parts of China and Russia. Their hands were tied.

At that moment, a young soldier, wearing all the regalia of a bureaucrat, not a warrior, entered and came up to Jong. "Mr. Prime Minister of the Cabinet, I have Admiral Ryu and Captain Sung Park standing by in the outer office."

Jong turned and looked out the window and then turned toward the group with a harsh look. "We must never forget, the American military in the Pacific are not the same as their political bureaucrats in Washington D.C. They can be a major obstacle to us. We must stay in touch with our new American friends we made during our negotiations."

Jong departed with the solider.

Chapter 11

Things had settled down at Polaris Point. Carla Kelly and seven members of her department entered Andy's Hut, the best place in the Pacific to get a cold beer after a tough day. Pittsburgh's weapons department had got all their stores and material down and stored for sea right before supper and Carla put the word out that she was buying.

As they entered, the place was rocking. Carla saw a group of tables where the USS Illinois crew members were drinking. Lieutenant Steve Garr was at the table head, being boisterous, obnoxious, and loud. There was one open table next to other Pittsburgh crew members and Carla and her team took it. Soon the barbs were flying as the sailors from Pittsburgh let off steam. Among members of Pittsburgh's weapons, engineering and operations departments, they were all giving as well as they got.

Steve Garr came over and stood directly behind and towering over Carla. He was a tall man, unshaven and, right now, well tanked. "Kelly, your ship was fucking lucky and you screwed us during the TRE."

Carla looked back at Steve. Smiling, she stood up, got on her chair and looked him right in the eye. "Lieutenant Garr, you stink. How you ever got through nuclear power school, I can't understand. Must have had a quota for football retards."

Steve Garr was so surprised by Carla that he initially stepped back and then got back into her face. "Fuck you, Kelly. Your CO is a fucking idiot and he's going to be thrown out of the submarine force."

Carla chuckled. "Well, I'm not sure he's a fucking idiot, but what does that make you – totally incompetent?"

With these words, the crewmembers at the Illinois table all stood and surrounded the Pittsburgh crew. At that moment, Drake and the COB entered and immediately saw what was brewing and walked over. As they approached, all the Illinois crew members, with the exception of Steve Garr, went back to their table.

Standing next to Carla and Steve, Drake calmly spoke. "What's going on here? Do we have a problem?"

Not waiting for an answer, the COB addressed Carla. "Lieutenant Kelly, I recommend you get your team's last beers down and get our people back to the ship."

Carla looked ashamed as she got down from her chair and sheepishly looked at the COB. "Yes COB." She called out to her team, "Guys, let's down those beers and get out of here."

The Pittsburgh sailors chugged their beers and started to leave.

Drake turned to Lieutenant Garr. "It's Lieutenant Steve Garr, isn't it?"

Garr was dumfounded that the commanding officer of the USS Pittsburgh knew his name. He slurred, "Yes sir."

"Well, it looks like you have a spirited group here. You need to get your team to start heading back too. Going into drydock is a dangerous experience and you will need to be sharp."

As the Illinois crew finished their beers and started to leave, the shore patrol showed up. Senior Chief Pitts, the team leader, came up to Drake. He knew exactly what had happened and was grateful he didn't have to do something that would cause a major disturbance.

"Captain Chandler, I am surprised to see you here. We just got called that there was trouble."

Drake looked at his crew leaving, then looked at Lieutenant Garr and back to Chief Pitts. "I don't think so, Senior

Chief. Looks like whatever might have happened has not come to fruition." Then, as an aside, he introduced Lieutenant Garr. "Oh, but by the way I'd like to introduce you to Lieutenant Garr, the weapons officer from the USS Illinois."

Chief Pitts was surprised. Garr, although drunk, understood that Captain Chandler had just saved him from serious trouble. He was at a loss for words and stuttered, "Y-y-yes, Senior Chief. We're all heading back to the ship."

Chief Pitts acknowledged, "Good idea."

With that, Garr turned to Drake. "Captain Chandler, it was a pleasure to meet you. I appreciate what you just did, and I hope your mission goes well." He then saluted and departed.

Chief Pitts watched the inebriated lieutenant depart and recognized that something had just happened. It reminded him of a past situation like the one he just observed. He turned back to Drake. "Captain Chandler, may I speak?"

Drake was surprised. "I normally don't get asked that, but yes."

Chief Pitts checked his shore patrol party and turned back to Drake. "I never got a chance to thank you for what you did for us on the Philly when we failed our Operation Rector Safeguard Examination."

Drake was surprised and slowly remembered. "You were the Reactor Controls LPO."

Chief Pitts smiled, marveling that Drake Chandler had remembered him. "Yes, sir. We weren't ready."

Drake's voice cracked with emotion as he responded. "No, Chief, you didn't fail your ORSE. Your squadron failed *you*. You weren't ready. They should have identified and helped you fix the issues that caused your failure. At least six other ships had had those same problems."

Chief Pitts was surprised. "All I remember was you were with us twenty-four hours a day for three weeks, helping us, and we passed the re-exam with flying colors. And none of it was due to the asshole deputy who took credit for our recovery. They didn't set foot on our ship, but made our captain go up and prostrate himself before the staff with mea culpas when he briefed them twice a day."

Drake was appreciative of these words. "Senior Chief, thank you for that compliment, but I was just doing my job." With that, Drake changed the subject. "What are you doing now, other than pulling periods of shore patrol duty?"

Chief Pitts smiled. "I'm with the squadron engineering staff. I'm trying to bring those skills you used with us for our ORSE recovery to the ships in the squadron."

Drake inwardly smiled, recognizing his efforts five years ago were paying off. "I'm so glad to hear that. Senior Chief, it is getting late and I need to head out."

Even though they were inside, Chief Pitts called his three-man team to attention, and they saluted as Drake departed.

The next morning, it was another beautiful, hot, sunny Guam day. Pittsburgh had been moved alongside the tender the previous day for final fitting out and all were preparing to get underway. A Mark VIII SEAL delivery vehicle and dry dock shelter had been lowered onto and secured to the midships hatch. Pittsburgh's advanced research and development mission had resulted in multiple demonstrations of the SDV and it was routinely stored on Pittsburgh. Additionally, Lt. Kelly had a team of ten Pittsburgh sailors who were qualified to operate the systems, including the COB, who was a pilot. With the tender deploying to the Philippines in the next two weeks, it was determined that Pittsburgh should take the SDV on its mission. It was going to spend the next three months at periscope depth of North Korea doing nothing. The general consensus was that there is no better place to get rid of the thing than on Pittsburgh.

Illinois was scheduled to depart the port side of the tender for the floating dry-dock at 0800. Pittsburgh would depart on its mission at 0900. A nice breeze made it comfortable on Pittsburgh, moored to the tender's westerly starboard side.

Pittsburgh's topside was a bustle of activity, as crewmembers were getting last-minute preparations done and cranes were pulling their shore power cables, removing off the trash container from the deck and hooking up to pull the brow.

On the tender's port side there was no breeze. It was hot in the early morning sun. Captains Sails and Prudsen were on the O-1 level, even with the Illinois bridge cockpit. On Illinois, Tom Witson was upset. He was ready to get underway, but he had no cranes to pull his shore power cables or his brow off his ship.

"Commodore, what's going on? I can't get in contact with the boatswains for cranes."

Stephan looked at Jerry Prudsen. "Jerry, find out what's going on."

Jerry shrugged his shoulders and set off to find the boatswains.

Drake Chandler and Captain Mains stood in Pittsburgh's bridge cockpit. Carla Kelly was OOD and she was talking with the pilot. As Carla looked down at the deck an older sailor with his sea bag and an envelope in his hands came running down the brow from the tender onto Pittsburgh.

The COB grabbed him when he stepped on onboard. "Hey, young man, just where do you think you're going?"

At that moment, the leading yeoman, YNI Tubbs, came aft from the port side of the sail and called out, "Hey, COB! He's our new CS. I just got a call from squadron ten minutes ago, letting me know they were sending him down."

The COB raised his hands in despair. "You've got to be shitting me."

Drake was surprised that the commodore was not there to watch his departure. He had made many departures, and the commodore was always there. He leaned over to Captain Mains. "Any idea where Commodore Sails is?"

Captain Mains gave him a sly grin. "I imagine he's over watching Illinois get underway, but with you having all three tender cranes tied up, I bet that is causing some difficulty."

Back on the tender's port side, Jerry Prudsen and a senior boatswain approached Stephan. Stephan, totally frustrated, unloaded. "Boatswain, where are the goddamn cranes that are supposed to be getting the shore power cables and brow off Illinois?"

The boatswain was not impressed and knew exactly why there were no cranes. "Sir, the crane crew captains are executing their orders as directed. Right now, they are all on the starboard side."

"What the hell do you mean? The Illinois was supposed to get underway forty-five minutes ago."

Tom Witson, listening to this exchange, exploded. "Why are the goddamn cranes not working my ship?"

The boatswain just shrugged his shoulders, knowing full well that Master Chief Mike Reinhardt, the Pittsburgh's COB, and their captain, Drake Chandler, went out of their way to support his teams and invited their families down for tours and weekend lunches. The Illinois crewmembers were a bunch of prima donnas and the worst was their captain.

Suddenly, there was one long blast from a ship's whistle, indicating a vessel was changing status from moored to underway. Stephan looked at Jerry and then at Tom Witson. "Fucking Chandler."

On the Pittsburgh, Carla looked back at Drake. "Sir, it's 0900, request permission to get underway."

Drake smiled. "Officer of the deck, get the ship underway."

Carla used the bullhorn to direct topside to put over all lines. It was always nice getting underway from your own home port, so you could use the tender's or pier's mooring lines, allowing you to keep you own mooring lines tied down in the free-flood stowage lockers. All a submarine needed was for a mooring line to get loose at sea and get caught in your propeller.

Carla turned to the pilot and requested him to have the tugs start pulling. As the alongside tugs pulled Pittsburgh away from the tender, Carla pushed the lever to sound one long blast on the ship's whistle.

Things settled down, and Captain Mains leaned over to Drake. "How much did you learn from Ops about what's going on in the Persian Gulf?"

"Enough to know it's right that we're the ones going there. We have far more remotely operated vehicle and underwater unmanned vehicle experience than any sub in the Navy. Without that, you have no chance against those bottom-hugging Iranian Ghadirs."

"I agree, but you've got a bigger problem. Commodore Sails and Captain Prudsen have a hate for you I just don't understand. As good as you and your crew are, you have alienated several influential senior officers in the Navy. Your mixed-gender fast attack puts a stick in their eye every time you succeed where others fail. Admiral Collar, who I highly respect and who has a fondness for you, needs to get Pittsburgh decommissioned because he sees Pittsburgh as too expensive to operate. That TRE performance severely pushed back his plans."

Drake was surprised at the frankness of Captain Mains' remarks. "That's unfair to Pittsburgh and even more so for Karen Young and Carla Kelly." Now agitated, Drake continued. "Those two are real talents who just demonstrated they are a significant cut above their peers. Every time they excel, guys like Johnson and Prudsen thwart their advancement and shuffle them off to dead-end jobs."

"Captain, that's just life in today's Navy. You have many supporters, but your run-in with Commodore Sails' father-in-law put the submarine force in jeopardy with high-ranking D.C. civilians. Worse yet, back on the east coast, Admiral Rentner and his band of staff sycophants put their personal status ahead of mission, and you are really rocking their boats. This Illinois drydocking is the only reason Commodore Johnson didn't relieve you of command, and the punitive letter, unfair as it is, will stick."

Drake looked glum. "Yes, sir. The Navy always sends me to the tough, ugly jobs. I salute, follow orders and solve their problems."

Captain Mains responded, "There's another problem."

Drake looked up in surprise.

"Do you know the president's national security adviser?"

"No. Should I?"

"Probably not, but she's talked to Commodore Sails and I understand she's tried to get hold of me. Evidently, she has a relationship with Sails."

Drake looked out over the harbor. "What's up?"

"Don't know, but it can't be good."

Drake looked down on the main deck as the COB and his topside team were rolling the cleats in and rigging topside for dive.

Captain Mains gave Drake an optimistic look. "At least you have a mission, even if its only surveillance off North Korea."

Drake shook his head. "Like that will add to my credentials." Derisively looking aft, he said, "I can see it now. Captain Chandler sat off the coast of the president's newest ally for three months and did nothing."

Captain Mains could see the pain in Drake's eyes. "Drake, that's your mission. You'll perform well as you always have. I can shield you for a while, but I am set to be relieved soon."

Drake was aware of this. "Yes, sir. That's been the story of my Navy career."

Ralph looked at him. "I know, but maybe this time you can change people's minds."

Drake shrugged. "And if I can't?"

Changing the subject, Captain Mains smiled. "But anyway, I am looking forward to meeting your crew and seeing how you run a 'mixed-gender' non-Virginia Class SSN."

Drake's spirits revived and, laughing, he looked at Captain Mains. "Commodore, you're going to learn quickly, bunking with the XO."

"Well, good. I'm heading below."

As Captain Mains departed, Carla made room for him to pass. She looked at Drake. "How bad it is Captain?"

Drake gave her a questioning eye. "I think the officer of the deck needs to keep her attention focused on getting us safely out of port."

Twenty minutes later, Drake was below, and Carla had cleared and rigged the bridge for dive. She stood on the conning stand, looking out number two periscope, as Drake and Captain Mains entered Control. The ship was preparing to do its initial dive after a period in port. This had potential for problems. Drake quietly asked, "How's it look, Officer of the Deck?"

Carla, keeping her eye on the scope, responded, "Captain, the shipped is rigged for dive and the compensation is entered." The compensation is an adjustment of water in variable tanks throughout the ship to provide a close proximity of neutral buoyancy when Pittsburgh submerged.

Drake nodded. "Officer of the Deck, submerge the ship."

Carla called out. "Diving Officer of the Watch, submerge the ship to 150 feet."

The diving officer repeated, "Submerge the ship, make my depth 150 feet, aye." To the chief of the watch, he ordered, "Sound the diving alarm."

Pittsburgh, like many of her older class of submarines, had been installed with a World War II vintage klaxon to replace the ugly electronic diving alarm. "Arugga! Arugga!" could be heard throughout the ship, followed by "Dive! Dive!"

The DOOW ordered, "Chief of Watch, open all main ballast tank vents."

The chief of the watch nodded. "Open all main ballast tank vents, aye." He then flipped the switches on the ballast control panel in front of him for the forward three main ballast tank vents, and their indicators turned from red bars to green circles. He then flipped the switches for the aft three main ballast tanks, and their indicators also turned from red bars to green circles.

Outside the ship, Pittsburgh moved easily through the

water, then a geyser of water shot up from the deck forward of the sail as the forward three main ballast tank vents opened. Shortly after that, a geyser of water shot up from the deck forward of the sail as the aft three main ballast tank vents opened.

Contrary to World War II submarines, the ship did not quickly submerge. World War II vintage only submerged to do their work or when they sighted enemy aircraft. They were small ships with large MBT vents to quickly get the air out of their ballast tanks and submerge, where modern submarines had small MBT vents as a matter of safety. No issue here. Pittsburgh wouldn't be on the surface again until they needed to surface to disembark Captain Mains and pick up the spook team in Japan. Inside the ship, the sound of the waves could still be heard lashing against the sail and moving through the free floods topside. Pittsburgh slowly started submerging.

The DOOW took control, smartly got the Pittsburgh to 150 feet and ordered all stop. Pittsburgh's speed started to slow from six knots. The DOOW ordered watered flood into the ship and pumped it to various fore and aft internal tanks. The planesmen used less and less fairwater or sail planes and stern planes to maintain depth. Finally, the ship slowed to less than one knot with zero angle on the fairwater and stern planes.

The DOOW tapped both planesmen on the shoulder. "Good job." He then leaned backward and announced, "At 150 feet and holding."

Pittsburgh had its initial reference trim that allowed them to perform thousands of daily evolutions that moved weight on, off and throughout the ship and still have a neutral buoyancy reference for the mission.

Chapter 12

With the ship submerged, below decks settled in on its usual peaceful calm with just the steady noise of air quietly whistling through the ventilation ducts.

Captain Mains was strolling through the mess decks. Culinary Specialist Senior Chief Roger Smith was walking among the tables filled with young sailors and officers taking examinations. Captain Mains motioned for Senior Chief Smith to talk with him at the back of the mess decks.

"What going on?" asked Captain Mains.

Senior Chief Smith beamed. "Sir, it's Thursday on Pittsburgh. That means anyone taking a written exam of any type must take it here, under my supervision. Even my mess cooks and CSs have to take written exams. The nukes and especially the officers have the four-hour tests, and they push us pretty hard getting the noon meal out."

Captain Mains and Lt. Smith looked back again at the mess decks. "Impressive, Senior Chief."

"Yes sir, no dinks on Pittsburgh."

Drake had called a mission brief in the wardroom at 1400. Most of the officers and key chief petty officers had crowded into the wardroom and awaited Drake.

Karen entered the wardroom with the message boards she had picked up in Radio and took her seat to the right of the captain's chair at the head of the table. Carla was in the seat next to her. The culinary specialists, including the older sailor who had just come aboard as the ship departed, were finishing getting coffee service set up for the briefing.

Carla leaned over. "What's the story with that old guy? I

see he's a CS."

Carla laughed. "Christ, he looks older than the COB."

Karen flipped to a new message. "The squadron called me just before we got underway and told me we were getting a new CS and, bingo, he shows up. Man, was Tubbs pissed."

Carla laughed. "Not only Tubbs, but I thought the COB was going to throw the guy overboard."

Karen flipped another message. "He's an interesting guy. He is a former submariner who left for several years and then came back into the service."

In the back of the wardroom, Captain Mains and the COB were talking. "COB, your ship looks great. I've seen brand new ships with little operating time that don't look this good and Pittsburgh has been to hell and back."

Mike Riner tried to be humble. "Thank you, sir. I don't know about the hell and back, but we have seen some serious operating time. But I will tell you, this ship is a direct reflection of her captain."

Ralph Mains put his hand on the COB's shoulder. "I know, but from my experience it takes a great COB to get this kind of performance."

At that moment Drake entered the wardroom. He walked over to Captain Mains and the COB. "Well, COB, have you been taking care of the good commodore?"

Ralph laughed. "He certainly has. I was just telling him how impressed I have been on my short time onboard."

"Well, thank you. It's all the result of the COB and his chiefs."

Mike Riner beamed.

Drake motioned to Ralph. "Captain Mains, please take a seat. We are interested in what you have to tell us."

Drake and Ralph took their seats and all others sat. The new CS put mugs of coffee in front of Drake and Ralph. Drake looked up at the older CS.

"I see it didn't take long for Chief Smith to get you into the job. Welcome aboard. It's Seaman Ames, correct?"

Ames was shocked and he looked around the wardroom. The captain knew his name and he'd been on board for less than four hours. "Yes, sir, and thank you, sir. I'm glad to be aboard." Ames went back to the pantry and closed the door.

Others around the table poured coffee into cups that had been laid out.

Captain Mains took a sip of coffee. "It great being back at sea – everything tastes better." He took another sip, relished the taste, and then leaned forward. "As you may know, Pittsburgh has been sent on a mission to conduct mandated monitoring of electronic transmissions and telecommunications off the coast of North Korea. Yes, North Korea is the president's newest ally, but Congress mandates this monitoring and they have demanded the president carry out the law. The submarine force hasn't done a lot of this mission since the end of the cold war. But for the next sixty days, Pittsburgh will be at periscope depth doing just that."

Carla shook her head. "Frickin' boring. You've got to be kidding me."

Captain Mains was a bit shocked at the lieutenant's quick tongue. "You'll be picking up a spook team of North Korean specialists in Yokosuka in three days to support your efforts."

Karen perked up. "Who will be the team leader. Do you know?"

Captain Mains gave her a quizzical look. "Interesting you ask, because that's surprising. I just learned this morning that your team will be led by a retired Navy limited-duty officer

99

commander named John Walker."

Karen gave a Spock-like smile. "Not necessarily a good name for a spook."

Thirty years earlier, a Navy chief warrant officer named John Walker and his son had given the Russians critical classified information that helped the Soviets decipher more than one million encrypted naval messages. That information had caused irreputable harm to numerous naval operations. Captain Mains, Drake and the COB were the only ones who got it, and they laughed.

Drake asked, "Why is that surprising?"

Ralph nodded. "Well, he and his team were supporting the president, his State Department and National Security teams on recent efforts with North Korea. I didn't think someone of that stature would be assigned to a mission like this."

Karen nodded. "I've read about him. He's a legend going back thirty years and a real rock star in the business."

Ralph sighed. "Yeah, and that will be a problem. Impressive, yes, but a huge pain in the ass. He thinks everybody should bow down and kiss his spook ring."

The COB laughed. "Well, sir, we can work on that with him."

Captain Mains looked at Carla. "Lieutenant, you're correct about the mission being boring, but at least there's a special added mission Admiral Collar and I want you to execute." Glancing at Drake, he went on. "Captain, we want you to conduct an enhanced underwater mapping of the North Korean continental shelf, just like you demonstrated in the tech eval of the new UUV system last year. The test results of those mappings sold the program."

Then looking at Carla, he added, "I had special UUVs covertly sent to you for that purpose but based on the special

UUV racks I saw in the torpedo room, something tells me someone knew they were coming."

Carla gave her cocky laugh. "Well, sir, I do sort of have a special relationship with the weapons staffs at the squadron and SubPac. You know: I help them, they help me."

Karen was troubled. "Commodore, I'm concerned this violates North Korean territorial waters. I'm not comfortable with that."

Drake responded, "Yes and no, XO. This is a congressionally mandated intelligence need, and our special unmanned underwater vehicle experience makes Pittsburgh the prime candidate to do this sort of mission."

Karen slowly shook her head. "I still think this does not comport with the Law of the Sea Convention."

Captain Mains finished his coffee and looked at Karen and Drake. "Captain Chandler, you will keep Pittsburgh outside twelve miles, but I want those UUVs to go in as far as possible and map as much of that area as they can." Then he devilishly smiled and said, "That should be easy, seeing that you'll be at periscope depth for the next two months."

Captain Mains was packing his bag in the XO's stateroom, and going over what he had observed in the last four days. The Pittsburgh was on the surface and it was rough. He heard the water crashing down the bridge access hatch and into the control room, which was just down the upper level passage from the XO's stateroom.

Pittsburgh had been on the surface for about six hours. The continental shelf off Japan was much like the eastern coast of the United States, where it went out for about sixty miles before most submarines would surface. The heavy seas and wind made it rough. With their rounded hull shapes, submarines didn't ride well on the surface in conditions like these. Water was seeping in under the stateroom door. He heard sailors trying to keep the water under control just outside the stateroom. He knew they were approaching the rendezvous point for the tug transfer.

The transit to Yokosuka had gone smoothly. The Pittsburgh crew quickly settled into their underway routine: training and written qualification exams in the morning; drills and battle station in the afternoon; and after the evening meal were movies in the mess decks and wardroom.

Ralph had observed a professionalism about this crew that he had not seen on other ships. On most submarines he rode, the crew rarely watch movies, especially the officers. Here there was always a movie in the mess decks and usually one in the wardroom. Officers and enlisted were getting their rigorous initial qualifications completed, but most of Pittsburgh's junior officers were all qualified in submarines and as nuclear engineers. Where most officers did not sit for the nuclear engineer examination until twenty-four months on board their first ship, somehow Drake Chandler got his officers through the grueling nuclear engineer qualification by the eighteen-month point.

His aide, Lieutenant Ed Robeson, had helped him understand why he had had this success. Lt. Robeson told him on his first ship he wasn't allowed to prepare for the ever-threatening Naval Reactor's Engineers Exam until he had been on board for two years. When he finally got a chance, he had extensively studied the reactor plant manuals and been interviewed by squadron and group staff officers who were supposed to get him ready. None of them were able to help him put things in perspective. It wasn't until his commanding officer had set up practice interviews with Captain Chandler that he finally figured it out.

Captain Chandler had a way of putting his interviewees in apparently simple situations that quickly got out of hand because they were responding to his probing questions with rote book knowledge and not thinking about what was happening to other parts of the reactor plant. He forced them to integrate what they had studied into common sense processes that weren't written in any book or manual. Captain Mains chuckled when he remembered Ed telling him Captain Chandler's favorite expression was "Now that you have violated reactor safety and possibly caused major damage, let's start over."

He was also impressed with Karen Young and the COB. She was the most – as her commanding officer called her – Spock-like officer he had ever met. She was cool and calculating, but with an empathy that made her invaluable and endeared her to the officers and crew. The COB lived up to his reputation as a man who knew how to invigorate the chiefs' quarters. Most COBs did that well, but Mike Riner was the best he had ever seen.

He finished packing his bag and noticed pictures taped to the cabinets above the desk, photos of Karen with a man and two young children. He heard people approaching outside the stateroom. There was a knock on the door and a moment later, Karen and Carla entered.

Karen was surprised. "Commodore, I'm sorry for interrupting."

Captain Mains smiled. "There are no interruptions on submarines." Then, looking at the pictures, he said, "XO, I didn't realize you had a family until I saw the pictures."

Karen was a little embarrassed. "That was taken just before David died five years ago."

Ralph was sorry he had asked. "I'm sorry. I didn't know. How do you support them when you're deployed?"

Karen was uncomfortable being reminded of this part of her life. "I've got great parents. They gave up their lives and moved in with me to help take care of the kids."

Carla, seeing Karen starting to tear, burst out, "And Karen's mom makes the best shoofly pie. It's like being home in Mississippi."

This broke Karen's dejection. "Yeah, and they're from small-town rural Indiana."

Ralph saw he had touched a nerve and responded, "There are many heroes supporting our military but ones like your parents never get recognized."

Karen felt a bit better. "Thank you, Commodore."

Ralph zipped up his bag. "I am glad we got a chance to meet before I depart. I am concerned for both of you."

Karen and Carla gave each other quizzical looks. Karen asked, "Why us?"

Ralph got serious. "Several things. First, Captain Chandler got you both here onto Pittsburgh by dubious backdoor channels. This burned bridges for both of you."

Karen became a bit upset. "I'm sorry sir, but that's bullshit. He saved my career from a dead-end job at Raytheon's missile division and brought me here for the Special Submarine Anti-Ballistic Missile Program."

Ralph was surprised by her emotional response. "My, you don't always act like Mr. Spock, as I've been told."

Carla was similarly concerned. "He brought me for the same reason, saving me from some jerk admiral who wanted to parade the pretty black submarine girl to show his 'diversity.'"

Ralph nodded in understanding. "I know that, but several influential people are still upset and his current status places you both in jeopardy. Senior bureaucrats are the most vindictive people I know."

Karen was having trouble fathoming all of this. "But we both were recognized and awarded medals for saving the Special Submarine Anti-Ballistic Missile Program."

Ralph knew these women didn't understand the background politics. "That program was supposed to fail. The Secretary of Defense didn't want to fund it and the president felt it was disruptive to his foreign policy initiatives. Your successes put the president in a difficult position with Congress."

Carla was shocked to hear this. "And then the bastards refused to take the missiles off! So now I'm the only fast-attack weapons officer with no vertical tomahawk launch capability."

Karen looked concerned. "This is related to the Captain Chandler and Undersecretary Benson affair, right?"

Captain Mains nodded.

"And we're going to pay for that!"

Captain Mains straightened. "Yes, and you've got to live with it. So, this mission is important to all of you. You must perform well. Senior people are looking for payback."

There was knock on the door and the COB entered. He observed the concern on Karen's and Carla's faces and recognized not all was well. "Excuse me. Commodore. We're ready topside. I'm here to get your bags."

Captain Mains nodded and a young sailor entered, picked up his bag and departed.

Chapter 13

Drake stood in Pittsburgh's cockpit. The winds and seas were up as Pittsburgh settled in on the lee provided by Izu Ōshima island just outside of Yokosuka. Still, a periodic wave came over the top of the bridge. He never like at-sea personnel transfers, but that was part of the job. Young Chris Pott had the deck and the conn, and he was staying on top of the many bad things that can happen in this evolution.

Waves were rolling over Pittsburgh's topside as a large tug came up on the lee provided by Pittsburgh. Even so, the tug lurched up and down with her rubber bumpers sliding up and down on Pittsburgh's hull. The COB and his topside crew, hooked into their safety track, moved to the tug, and were taking on last-minute provisions and equipment from the tug. Most of the boxes were support equipment for the spook team. As always, there were fresh provisions, milk, fruit, eggs – things that would be gone in a week but nice to have. The key for this evolution was to time the waves and make transfers on the steady high pitch of the tug before it descended back down.

On the tug, forty-four-year-old, crusty, heavily pockmarked Retired Limited Duty Officer Commander John Walker and his team were standing by to board to Pittsburgh. John Walker had done these many times early in his career, but that was twenty years ago. He had forgotten how dangerous this was. Right now, he was on a satellite phone with Susan Grains in Washington D.C. It was certainly a one-way conversation. "Yes, Susan. Yes, Susan. Yes, Susan. I fully understand. I've heard about Chandler and I will make sure he does nothing stupid."

Susan was adamant as she went on about this USS

Pittsburgh not subverting what they had put in place just two months ago with the president's "Peace in Our Time" negotiations. She told him the United Nations was ecstatic, and overwhelmingly passed its approval, with the only holdouts being Japan, South Korea, the Philippines, Vietnam, India, and Australia. As she ranted, John didn't listen. He was still pissed off that she had screwed up everybody's time off after the night and day negotiations in North Korea by making him and his team ride Pittsburgh.

John finally got a word in edgewise, thanked Susan for her compliments and acknowledged he had enjoyed his time working with her in Pyongyang. In fact, Susan proved to be a tiger in bed. John knew she did this with anyone she thought she needed to control but he had enjoyed the ride anyway.

As John Walker and his team boarded Pittsburgh, one junior member slipped on the hull and a muscular topside team member grabbed him by his coat collar and put him face down on the deck like he was nothing. At that moment, the large tug coming down off a wave would have crushed him.

Captain Mains, the last man to depart, looked up at Drake at the top of the sail. "Good luck, Captain. I'd say something about fair winds and following seas but today that seems inappropriate."

Drake laughed. "You know, if you don't make the Leap for Life you may be on this mission with us."

With that, Ralph expertly timed his jump and easily stepped onto the tug rail, then onto the tug's main deck. Once the provisions and personnel were down, the COB and sailors rigged topside for dive and Pittsburgh headed back to sea.

Chief Smith met the team as they arrived below decks and escorted them to their bunks. He informed them they needed to be in the wardroom in about five hours. Many of the team were not used to being at sea on a ship the rolled and bucked like Pittsburgh on the surface. Most dove into their bunks to fight off seasickness. Four hours later, a young sailor pulled their bunk curtains back and told them they were needed in the wardroom.

Karen and key Pittsburgh crew members were in the wardroom, welcoming John Walker and his team of intelligence specialists. It was still rough, and the ship was preparing to dive. Suddenly, there were two blasts of the diving klaxon and over the 1MC blared, "Dive! Dive!" It took a while, but eventually the ship steadied into the peaceful calm of a submarine submerged.

Doc, HM2 Amanda Rothlein, had got all their medical records and issued dosimetry. YN1 Tubbs picked up their records so he could process their ride time. In the coroner, RMC Rita Belt was talking up John Walker like they were old friends.

Drake entered the wardroom, still wet from having been on the bridge just before diving. Starting with John Walker, he went to each spook team member and shook their hands. John Walker watched the man. He knew each of their names and mentioned something about their history. This guy was not the dunderhead Susan Grains had described.

Finally, Drake said, "Gentlemen, welcome. Why don't we take a seat? I need some hot coffee."

As soon as Drake had had several sips he commented, "Gentlemen, welcome aboard the Pittsburgh. Sorry for our little delay. I assume the XO, COB and crew have made you welcome."

John nodded. "Thank you. They have. I haven't been on a submarine operation in over twenty years." With a cocky look, he said, "And to tell the truth, I was a little surprised my team got pulled off a well-deserved break to come out here and babysit you."

Karen was offended. "Babysit? Did you really say that?"

John was caught off guard. "My apologies, ma'am. I am sorry. Did not mean it that way, but I am the premier cryptologic technician specialist in the Navy and I'm not sure why I need to be here."

Drake rolled his eyes and looked at Karen and the COB, and commented, "The submarine force hasn't done this type of mission for many years."

John smiled. "Well, I have been doing this my entire Navy career. I'll let you know how it's done."

Again, Drake couldn't get over the conceit in Walker. "Thank you for that, Mr. Walker. So, I guess that's part of the babysitting?" Drake gave Karen a look of concern. "XO, please discuss ground rules with Mr. Walker and his team."

Karen looked at each team member. "Now, the first thing we want to emphasize is that we are a mixed-gender SSN. In fact, we are the only non-Virginian Class mixed-gender SSN, and the oldest and only non-688i class submarine in the fleet. A great submarine class designed when there were no thoughts of women on submarines. We do not have the space of our ballistic missile and SSGN submarine brethren or the female spaces on the newer Virginia Class. That raises some issues for those who don't understand working in the close quarters we have on Pittsburgh."

Drake thought he saw a level of contempt in the eyes of the members of the spook team. He said, "That is not a problem as long as you buy into Pittsburgh's philosophy about the crew and any riders." With added emphasis he continued, "And you don't have a choice. On Pittsburgh, you look at your shipmates as blood brothers and sisters; or for me, the XO and possibly Mr. Walker, as our sons and daughters. This is the standard!"

Drake and Karen saw some internal snickering from team

members, but John Walker kept a straight face. Drake continued, "Gentlemen, please look me in the eye as I say this. There is zero tolerance with respect to sexual misconduct on my ship. In my first two weeks in command I court martialed a lieutenant commander and first-class petty officer for sexual misconduct. I am not some cruiser captain playing politics. I would not think more than a second about doing the same to you."

The spook team members looked around to find someone who might support them.

Drake waited for their comments. "Do you understand? And I would like to see each of you nod your heads acknowledging that understanding."

Each of the team members grudgingly nodded agreement.

At that moment, John Walker broke in. "Captain, I am normally referred to as commander because of my former rank in the Navy."

This comment caused the COB's head to jerk up, and he looked at him condescendingly. The COB parried Walker's remark with, "Thank you for your service Mr. Walker, but on Pittsburgh the only commanders are the executive officer and the engineer."

John Walker looked at Drake. "Then you aren't a commander."

Karen decided to put an end to this. "Mr. Walker, are we going to have salutation issues?"

John Walker did not like that put-down, but he held it in. "No, ma'am."

Drake stood up and prepared to leave. "Good. Now that we've addressed that, the XO will go over your team's qualification and examination program for your time on board."

As he opened the wardroom door, John Walker

interrupted. "Captain, we've got to set up our equipment and get ready."

Drake nodded consent. "Good idea. But nobody on this ship does anything without some form of qualification. You can do your preps on your own time."

John Walker indignantly stiffened. "Captain, that's not the way I operate."

Drake shut the door and turned to face Walker. "Mr. Walker, you appear to be a man with issues. Are there going to be more?" Drake paused and looked at Karen. "If so, I am sure that the XO and you can deal with it. While on Pittsburgh, you work for me."

PART THREE – NORTH KOREAN WATERS

Chapter 14

Pittsburgh headed southeast through the Philippine Sea, then turned west into the East China Sea before shooting the Korean Strait into the Sea of Japan.

Drake had taken his time letting his crew and the spook team have some time working together to get their operations smoothed out. Pittsburgh's plan was to start at the southern end of North Korea near the port town of Koson and slowly transit north to the Russian-North Korean border, then reverse course. He concluded that would provide the electronic transmissions coverage and provide a good mapping of the continental shelf.

Drake had not slept since they had left Guam. His punitive letter was a death sentence to his career. There would be no rank of captain in his future and only a series of dead-end jobs would follow. Depressed, emotionally torn, beaten down and morose, he spent a lot of time sitting in his stateroom in the tee shirt and gym shorts he used for sleeping, with only his desk lamp providing illumination. This morning, he sat reading his punitive letter of reprimand for the umpteenth time. Pictures of his wife, Laura, and his three smiling kids, were taped to the doors over the desk.

Earlier in the day, they had picked up some distant active sonar activity. No doubt the North Koreans were conducting some form of ASW training. Drake was sure of that and he intended to stay well out of the way. Drake looked at the sonar display at the right of his desk. Some disturbing traces showed them coming his way.

The 2JV phone screeched next to the desk. It was the officer of the deck. Drake put down the letter and, chameleon-like, transformed himself into an energetic, thoughtful, charismatic leader and picked up the phone handset. As he listened, he nodded his head in agreement.

Carla was the OOD, and Drake responded. "I concur. I have no idea what the North Koreans are up to. Tell the exec to come and get me when she has the situation laid out on the geo plot."

He looked at his sonar display again. Carla said something over the phone. Drake responded, "Very well, make preparations to go to periscope depth. Prepare to blow sanitaries."

Drake hung up the phone and his demeanor returned to troubled. He picked up the letter, frustration in his face. He pounded his desk and an emotional tear rolled down his cheek.

There was a knock on the door. Drake recovered his composure, put the document in a desk drawer and locked it. After a few seconds, Karen entered.

"Captain, I've got the plot ready."

Drake stood. "Thanks, XO. I'll be out in a minute."

Karen looked suspiciously at the desk and left.

Outside, the COB was waiting. He was concerned. "How's the old man?" He had never seen his captain like this.

Karen shook her head. "Still keeps looking at that letter."

The COB shook his head. "Sails really screwed him this time. He may not survive."

Karen gave a frustrated look. "No shit. My fear is the impact on Pittsburgh and us."

The COB shook his head. "XO, Captain Chandler won't let anything happen to us."

Karen frowned. "That assumes he has any control."

The CO's stateroom door opened, and Drake stepped out. He gave a dubious look at Karen and the COB, then looked up at the ventilation duct above his door and smiled.

"You know, for two supposed seasoned submarine veterans like yourselves, you ought to know how thin these bulkheads are. Now, why don't you two not worry about me and get on with your jobs." He paused a beat. "XO, let's see what you've got."

As part of preparing to blow sanitaries, the auxiliaryman of the watch was in the lower level head, hanging "blowing sanitaries" signs, putting wires on the toilet bowl flush valves to keep them from opening when waste water was blown off the ship.

A man approached. "Hey man, I really got to piss."

The auxiliaryman nodded and pointed to one stall. "OK, but make sure when you're done you reset the wires and re-hang the sign."

As the auxiliaryman departed, the man entered the stall, removed the wire from the flush valve, pulled the lever to open the toilet, and dropped a plastic ball into the tank below it. He shut the valve, reset the blowing sanitaries sign and wire, and departed.

Back in Control, Drake and Karen entered, stopping at the geographic plot. ASW active sonar pings could be heard from the sonar speakers.

Karen leaned over the plot and started laying out the picture. "Here there are several North Korean warships, ASW helicopters and ASW VP aircraft searching maybe 15.7 miles North of us."

At that moment three multi-frequency sonar transmission come over the control sonar speaker.

Drake looked up. "Interesting. They rarely conduct ASW exercises."

Karen stood up. "Yeah, but what bothers me is they are right in our mission area."

Drake smirked and shook his head. "At least they're not very good at it."

He strolled over to the conn area of the control room and observed the sonar display. Carla was busy checking her instruments and indications for coming to periscope depth. Drake looked at the several displays. "Weps, do you normally let your sonar supe skip details?"

Carla gave Drake a smiling and overconfident look. "No, sir. I'd kill him if he ever did that."

Drake saw a teaching moment and pointed to the sonar display. "Don't kill him now, but how many ships are out there?"

As Carla looked at the display, a pissed look came over her face. She started to take off for the sonar shack. "I'm going to kill that son-of-a-bitch," she said.

Drake put his arm out, stopping her. Carla pulled back and Drake looked at her. "Not now. It's pretty busy in Sonar. Once you get off watch, you pull him aside and hold him accountable." Drake sat down in his chair. "Let's get to PD."

On the ocean surface, fifteen miles to the north of Pittsburgh, three North Korean corvettes and two frigates were conducting ASW, or at least what they thought was ASW.

Admiral Ryu and Captain Sung Park looked out over their ASW flotilla. Lots of random active sonar transmission and reactions to nothing, or false returns from the bottom and scattering filled their displays. A helicopter lifted off one of the frigates and two VP patrol aircraft were to the south of the little flotilla, dropping sonar buoys and flying low to conduct magnetic anomaly detection, or MAD runs. It was a bit of controlled chaos.

On Pittsburgh, Carla turned to Drake. "Sir, I've completed all preparations for going to periscope depth. I have no close contacts. Request permission to proceed to PD."

Drake, sitting in his chair, looked one more time at the conn sonar display. "Proceed to periscope depth. When ready, blow sanitaries."

"Aye, sir." Carla called out, "Diving officer, make your depth sixty-two feet."

Carla raised the periscope. As the scope broke the surface, Carla quickly moved the scope clockwise. Electronic surveillance monitoring chirps came through the ESM speaker. Carla called out, "No close contacts." She then slowed her clockwise search and conducted a thorough search. "I've completed an initial search and no contacts. Diving officer of the watch, blow sanitaries."

Outside of Pittsburgh, along the hull, water started emanating from a sanitary tank overboard on the submarine side. A plastic ball came out of the overboard hole and rose to float on the surface. On the surface the ball opened, and a small antenna protruded from the middle.

Back in Control, the normal reports and activities of getting to periscope depth continued. ESM reported, "Conn, ESM, I hold two probable North Korean VP aircraft and three probable ASW helos. General bearing of north."

At that moment, a loud deafening steady screech came from the ESM speaker. Concern showed on Drake's face. Karen

116

came onto the conn.

Drake stood and look up into the open mike. "ESM, what's that?"

"Captain, ESM, I have no idea, but whatever it is, it's close."

Drake looked at Karen. "XO, get into ESM and see what the hell that is."

On the ASW flotilla flagship, Admiral Ryu and Captain Sung Park were talking on the bridge when the command phone squawked. Captain Park answered. An excited voice almost screamed, "Commodore! We have intercepted our locator beacon and have triangulated the location twenty-five kilometers bearing 163 degrees!"

Commodore Park quietly nodded. "Very well, direct our southerly VP aircraft to launch an attack at that location."

Admiral Ryu had heard the discussion and nodded his concurrence. "Well, our intelligence was quite accurate. We need to get there quickly so our torpedoes have a chance to hit the target."

Back on Pittsburgh, a change in the sonar transmissions came over the sonar open speaker, followed by the sonar supervisor's voice. "Conn, Sonar, something has happened! The North Korean ships are maneuvering. Best guess is they are turning toward."

Drake tapped Carla on the shoulder and took over the scope. "Let's take a high look." He adjusted the diopter and rotated the scope. "Diving officer, make your depth five zero feet."

The diving officer called out his depths. "sixty feet, fifty-five feet, fifty feet and holding, sir."

Drake scanned the area to the north. "Mark this bearing."
The quartermaster called out "3-4-8."
Drake move the scope slightly clockwise. "Mark this bearing."
"0-0-9."
Rotating the scope slightly clockwise, "Mark this bearing."
"0-1-5," responded the quartermaster.
Drake nodded to Carla, who came and took over the scope and spoke, then called out, "Diving officer, make your depth sixty-eight feet."
As Karen returned to Control, Drake moved to the geo plot and spoke to the entire control area. "I held a group of ships very distant to the northwest. I called off bearings to the three closest airborne contacts. The first mark was a distant hello dipping its sonar. The second a VP aircraft coming right at Pittsburgh."
Looking at the plot, Karen commented, "It was definitely a locator beacon, but how did it get next to us?"
Drake looked off into space, as he often did when thinking. "This is not good." After a short pause, he turned to go into Sonar. "XO, take the scope. WEPS, maintain the deck and come with me to Sonar."
Even though they were not at battle stations, Sonar was crowded. The sonar supervisor, and the four panel operators in front, were being squeezed by the COB, the sonar chief, and now Drake and Carla.
The COB looked at Drake. "Captain, these guys are pinging and searching like a chicken with its head cut off. No discipline or technique."
The sonar supervisor piped up. "And, sir, we saw a torpedo out to the north a while ago."
Drake nodded to the supervisor. "The torpedo – a poor

118

man's search technique. Most submarines, if they hear a torpedo in the water, they panic and give themselves away."

The sonar chief pointed to a set of lines on a sonar panel. "In fact, there's a VP aircraft approaching, and I think he's going to drop sonobuoys."

Drake nodded. "I see it." He looked at the COB. "Take the dive and be ready."

The COB departed.

Four miles north of Pittsburgh, a low-flying ASW aircraft dropped a pattern of sonobuoys. In Sonar, the active sonobuoys were heard as they started pinging.

Carla looked at Drake, "My God, these guys aren't this good, how'd they find us?"

"They had help." Drake nudged the sonar supervisor and pointed to a display.

The supervisor looked and said, "Yes sir, looks like a second VP aircraft is coming around for a torpedo drop."

Three miles north of Pittsburgh, a low-flying VP aircraft flying directly at Pittsburgh released a torpedo. The torpedo dropped into the water and its motor started. It actively started pinging, circled, and turned toward Pittsburgh. A sonar operator jumped abruptly. "Supervisor, just picked up a torpedo in the water, bearing 3-5-7."

A sonar screen panel brightened as torpedo motor lines appeared. "Looks like a Chinese YU-7 ASW torpedo series."

As the sonar supervisor picked up the mike to call away the torpedo, Drake stopped him. "Do not call away that torpedo."

Everyone in Sonar turned and looked at Drake in horror. Drake tapped Carla on the shoulder, and they departed.

As they came into Control, Karen was on the scope. Active torpedo pings could now be heard on the control room sonar speaker. Ping…ping…ping. It was obviously in a search mode.

Drake walked to the bathythermograph. There was a thermal layer just below 120 feet. "This is the captain. I have the conn. COB, make your depth 1-6-3 feet, fast. On the helm, come right to course 3-2-7."

With a down angel coming on the ship, Karen lowed the scope. In the background there was ping…ping…ping…ping…ping.

In Control, a sense of fear and tension developed. As the ship decreased depth, the COB called out. "7-0 feet, 8-0 feet, 9-0 feet, one hundred feet, 1-2-5 feet, 1-5-0 feet."

The pings were louder but still steady. Drake called out, "All stop. Back one third."

The helmsman rang up his orders on the engine order telegraph. The COB announced "One-six-three feet and holding."

As Pittsburgh leveled and its headway came off, the torpedo turned toward and started to range-gate on Pittsburgh. Ping…ping…ping…ping…ping…ping…pingpingpingpingping. From the conn sonar speaker came, "Conn sonar, the torpedo has locked onto and is homing on Pittsburgh."

Throughout Control, sailors tensed with a sense of terror. Drake observed his speed decreasing from two knots to zero knots.

"All stop. Dive, I want you to hover at this depth."

The COB turned around and looked at Drake. "You know, sir, this is a bit tough with no speed."

Drake, upset with his comment, said, "COB, you're supposed to be the best diving officer on the damn ship, so don't tell me you can't do the job. Just do it!"

The pings became louder. PINGPINGPINGPING! Outside

the ship, the torpedo was just off the starboard bow and closing Pittsburg's position. Inside the ship, the torpedo propellers could be heard. The pings were deafening. Several crew members started to shake, and some developed tears in their eyes. Pittsburgh's speed finally stopped at zero.

Outside the ship, the torpedo pings started to come at longer intervals as it lost contact. PINGPINGPING-PING-PING-PING...PING...PING...PING. The torpedo altered course to starboard and passed directly ahead of Pittsburgh, and disappeared down the port side as it continued to search. "Conn sonar, the torpedo stopped ranging and returned to search mode."

Carla walked over next to the geographic plot and its team. "Damn, that took fuckin' balls!"

The COB leaned over to Drake. "My guess is, that wasn't an exercise torpedo."

Drake shook his head in disbelief. "That was to stimulate us into doing something stupid."

Throughout the control room, tension diminished. As active sonars faded in the background, Drake spoke. "Ladies and gentlemen, I think the North Koreans just gave it their best shot. If they'd ever got us, they'd have been all over us until we were on the bottom."

Drake moved to the geo plot and looked at the total picture. His team had the interaction well laid out. He called out, "Lieutenant Kelly has the deck and the conn. Officer of the deck, clear out to the east at best speed for this depth for the next hour, then give me a call."

He looked at Karen and the COB. "Get Walker and be in my stateroom in five minutes."

Drake was sitting at his desk when there was a knock. A moment later the door opened and Karen, the COB and John

Walker entered. The COB was obviously upset.

"Captain, there is no way the North Koreans could have done that well. They had to have been tipped off."

"I totally agree. But how?" He looked at John. "Mr. Walker, have you ever seen anything like that?"

John shook his head. "No, sir. That was strange. I was in Radio, right next to the ESM gear. There was a transmitter that just started up. I think it had to have come from within the ship."

Drake rubbed his face with his hand in a thoughtful moment. "We need to let SubPac and Group Seven know. But off the coast of North Korea, we're going to have to use the Submarine Special Intelligence Communications Network to do it. That means it goes to the D.C. wienies, who will see it before those who really understand."

Karen looked Drake in the eye. "Captain, I think we need to clear the area until we figure this out."

Drake shook his head. "No! We'll clear to the east till the North Koreans get tired and then get back on station and start executing our mission."

Karen stood her ground and challenged Drake. "But, Captain, this isn't the attack trainer. That was a real torpedo!" She raised her voice. "We're talking about the lives the crew and our families. What about all that values stuff you always preach?"

The COB stepped in. "XO, that's not fair."

Karen looked at the COB, then at Drake. "Oh, yeah?"

Drake had to end this squabble. "XO, right now I want you to get Weps preparing our UUVs, and then you and Mr. Walker need get into the books and find out what that electronic screeching noise was."

Chapter 15

Pittsburgh's message had made its way through all the special intelligence communications channels and finally to the NSA. Susan smiled as she thought how well her little arrangement with Mr. Jong had gone. Now she could push these bureaucrats to get rid of a major obstacle to the president's initiative. More importantly, this could make it possible for the president to win the Nobel Peace Prize. These people are idiots. We're were getting the North Koreans to give up their nuclear weapons. He would accomplish what neither of his two predecessors had achieved.

Susan had gathered the president's chief of staff, Clark James, SecDef Tom Reynolds, SecNav Judith Wilson, and Chief of Naval Operations Admiral Gensen in the White House Situation Room. James was on board, but Reynolds and Wilson were fighting it. Of course, they were the ones who could be called before Congress and get beat up on matters like this. She hoped Admiral Gensen might push them to get the Pittsburgh off the coast of North Korea.

Susan entered the secure conference room. As she took her seat at the head of the table, she saw them reviewing the message from Pittsburgh. She observed, "I see our submarine got roughed up a bit. If something had happened during that encounter, it could have destroyed the Peace in Our Time Initiative."

Tom Reynolds looked over at her. "Yeah, I see the commanding officer reported that North Korean ASW operations were being conducted just as they arrived on station. That was certainly strange."

Seeing her opportunity, she jumped in. "This is the kind of thing that can cause an international incident, and the commanding officer of that submarine has serious issues. I think we use this message as the ammunition to get that sub out of there."

Admiral Gensen put his copy of the message down. "Madam Director, the commanding officer may have some issues, but it sounds like his ship performed well. He noted the effort was poorly organized and he is proceeding on to conduct his mission."

Susan gave the Admiral a harsh look. "Admiral, I don't care. I want him out of there."

Finally, Clark James stepped in. "Susan, as we discussed before, politically we can't do that right now. Congress is pissed, as are many senior officers in the Pentagon. If Congress saw what the North Koreans did, they might dig in even deeper."

Susan saw she had lost this battle, but got the last threat in. "Admiral Gensen, you'd better hope your submarine commander doesn't go off the reservation. If he does, I will assure you, your career is over."

Chapter 16

Pittsburgh had cleared the area and played possum for twelve hours after the torpedo attack. The North Koreans stopped searching, and their ships and aircraft soon left. Karen and John Walker had reviewed past mission reports and intelligence info and could find nothing like what had just happened to Pittsburgh. Drake was concerned that one of his newly arrived crewmembers or riders was not who he was supposed to be.

Drake stayed in Control as the ship proceeded to the initial starting point. They had been at periscope depth for the last six hours. The terror that had accompanied the torpedo firing had mostly dissipated. Crew members talked about it but not with the intensity of the moment when the torpedo had locked on. Drake, finally overcome by lack of sleep and the recent minutes of terror, went to his stateroom, and crashed on his bunk for some much-needed sleep.

In Control, Karen was talking with the operations officer, Lt. Mike Miller. The OOD was coordinating the raising and lowering of communication masts. The team work between the spooks and the ship's control parties was settling in. In Radio, spook team members were installing equipment into communications racks and conducting final calibrations of equipment.

When Drake awoke from his nap, he proceeded to the torpedo room. There, Carla and TM1 Pender were looking at the UUVs and the support equipment.

Carla pointed out to Drake the four UUVs she had brought onboard. They were not Navy production models in the Navy Master Plan – those were several years away. These were off-the-shelf UUVs that had been demonstrated on Pittsburgh when Carla worked at the Submarine Development Squadron.

"Captain, I intend to get the UUVs out through trash disposal unit, and their fiber-optic cable assemblies out of the torpedo tubes. The torpedo tube deployment is too difficult and dangerous for my divers. We'll align their inertial navigators in the TDU room and hook up their fiber cables in the water as they exit the TDU."

"That's not what the manual says."

Carla chuckled. "I know, but that manual assumes I am on a Virginia Class or 688i and not a Second Flight 688. You told me to make sure we are successful the first time. This is far simpler, and it's how our crew was trained."

Drake nodded his approval. He knew the dangers of diving next to a submarine while in port, but they were doing it at sea off a foreign coast. There were no backups if things went wrong. "Good, let's make sure you go over all the safety issues with your team. Diving next to a submarine at PD is not the safest thing in the world."

Three hours later, Carla and TM1 Pender were in wet suits below the Pittsburgh, as a torpedo-shaped UUV emerged from a large hole in the hull. A third diver approached, pulling a thin fiber cable in a loop. He handed the cable to Carla, who took the free end and installed it in the UUV. They had accomplished this maneuver a thousand times.

Carla pressed her underwater communicator. "Smith continuity test."

In the torpedo room, FT2 Smith made several adjustments to the stand-alone UUV control laptop and sent the test pulse. At the UUV cable connector, Carla saw the three test lights start to blink and then go steady. Carla communicated "Test Sat." She then pushed the UUV away the port side of Pittsburgh. The UUV's propellers started and the UUV moved on its own.

Carla tapped Pender on the shoulder indicating she was going back on board. As she left a second UUV came down out of the TDU.

Back on board, Carla went to Control. In the background, discussions could be heard between Control and the spook team in the radio room about intercepts made and requests to raise the direction-finding masts. Carla saw Karen and Drake observing the initial mapping pictures being received from the first UUV. They were quite remarkable.

Karen motioned them all to the geographic plot, where she had set up grids to track the UUVs mapping progress. Each UUV had about 10,000 yards or five nautical miles of fiber cable. Pointing to the bottom of the grid map, she commented, "I have us here on the map, and we'll let the UUVs work their way back and forth through these grids. With the currents, we'll have to bottom the UUVs daily to let their gyros and accels realign. Every third day, we will need to bring them alongside to charge their batteries and get a fine align with the ship's inertial navigator."

Drake looked at the map. "Weps, how did you phrase it? 'Frickin' boring.'"

With the UUVs deployed and mapping, Pittsburgh stayed at periscope depth for three weeks, listening for North Korean communications and monitoring any military radar or other transmissions.

Drake was finally starting to get some sleep, but when he did, it was fitful, and he frequently woke up to nightmares. He couldn't shake the punitive letter of reprimand that sat in his locked drawer. When he couldn't sleep, he would roam the ship, often spending time in the engineering spaces, where the steam noise and sound of running machinery were comforting to him. Beside his punitive letter, the lack of any form of North Korean communications was of real concern. Since they had arrived on station three weeks earlier, all electronic transmissions had ceased.

After evening meal, Drake and Karen went to Radio/ESM. John Walker was reviewing logs and writing his daily report. One spook team member and RM2 Sanchez were logging traffic and observing receivers from the various electronic stacks. It was pretty quiet.

As Drake went over the recent radio traffic, his frustration got to him. "XO, so much for a great mission – three weeks, and nothing. We've been here for three fucking weeks, and nothing."

Karen picked up the frustration with concern. "Yes, sir."

Drake threw his message board down and ranted under his breath to Karen. "We arrive on station, get attacked, and now zero electronic transmissions."

Drake walked over to John Walker. "Mr. Walker, what do you make of this? Are you seeing any activity out there?"

"None, sir, other than some small fishing boat radars. When I was here just last year, there was always some form of radar transmissions and communications."

Drake threw his hand up. "Jesus Christ, we're twelve miles off the coast of North Korea near some of their largest and most important military facilities, and you're telling me we're seeing no activity."

"Yes, sir. I've been doing this for twenty years and it has never been like this."

Drake had had enough and started to leave. He looked back at Karen. "XO, we're screwed."

As Drake made his way back to his stateroom, the COB saw a new pain in his captain's face. He followed and entered Drake's stateroom right behind him. Once Drake was in his stateroom, he turned toward the COB just entering and slapped the wall in defeat.

In a ranting emotional outburst, Drake erupted. "I'm fucked! Pittsburgh's fucked! We don't get the Persian Gulf mission and now we bust our asses to do everything perfectly and we have nothing."

Drake flopped into his chair. "There's no way Pittsburgh survives the scrap yard after this piece-of-shit mission."

The COB closed the door and gave Drake a tough look and admonished him. "Captain, you've got to knock this sniveling stuff off and suck it up. I don't care how much shit you are in." He moved right in front of Drake and looked him in the eye. "You can't even look that way. Every man and woman in this crew looks to you for inspiration. They live and breathe knowing you are their commanding officer, and they'll follow you to hell and back and love it."

Drake was having none of it. "Screw you, COB. Your career's not on the line. You're set up for SubPac Command Master Chief anytime you want it."

The COB was not ready for that and put on his I'm-the-toughest-man-on-this-ship attitude. "Don't give me that bullshit, sir! This is my ship too, and I live and die with it. I know all about them taking your command away, but acting like this isn't going to help."

The harshness and truth of the COB's words finally registered, and Drake recovered from his tantrum and looked ashamed. Putting his hands on his knees and looking at the deck he

apologetically responded. "Master Chief, I know what I have to do." Waiting a minute and
thinking, he looked up at the COB. "And COB – thank you."

Chapter 17

Thirty-eight miles to the northwest of Pittsburgh, Jong Song was meeting with his staff. Preparations for the upcoming nuclear missile launch were proceeding well, but he was still upset, having expected his navy to have sunk the goddamn submarine after he had pinpointed it for them.

Again, he felt he was surrounded by incompetents. Men who rose to positions of power through nepotism and bribery. He was exasperated by their failure. He cruelly looked at Admiral Ryu and Captain Park. "I gave you a locator beacon and the exact position of this submarine and you failed to sink it. How could you fail to find this submarine Pittsburgh?"

Commodore Ryu looked at Captain Park to pass the blame onto him. Captain Park spoke in his own defense. "We were at the position you provided when we detected the beacon. But then our sonars and sonobuoys could not find the submarine. We even put a war shot torpedo right on top of the locator beacon."

Mr. Song stopped him by waving his hand. He stood up. "Don't patronize me, Captain. You failed."

Commodore Ryu spoke up. "Mr. Song, sir, this USS Pittsburgh Commanding Officer, a Commander Drake Chandler, he is evidently some form of what the Americans call a 'maverick.'"

Mr. Song sneered. "And why do I care?"

"I just thought it interesting. He may present a problem."

Mr. Song was now incensed. "Commodore, your job is to make sure I have no problems!"

At that moment, an aide entered with a telephone. "Mr. Song, sir, you have a call from the American presidential advisor,

Madam Grains."

Jong took the phone and turned to Ryu and Park. "Admiral, find out more about this Chandler. We need to find a weakness."

Jong changed to his smoothest, sincerest voice. "Susan, how good to hear from you. How is your day going?"

"Not well, but thank you for asking. Our submarine off your coast reported your antisubmarine warfare efforts, but it also reported a torpedo being used. That didn't go over well." She paused "I only asked you to harass him."

Jong smiled. "I am so sorry. It was stupid. But you know military officers – always wanting to use their toys. I have chastised my people for their failure to obey my explicit orders to not use any form of weapon."

Jong heard the note of satisfaction in Susan's voice as she said, "Thank you. Of course, right now I'm unable to get the Navy to remove the submarine."

Jong was not happy. "I appreciate your efforts Susan. We are not happy having a U.S. submarine off our coast, but we will monitor its presence."

Susan said thank you and disconnected the line.

When Jong hung up, he looked at Ryu and Park. "I want that submarine found and sunk. Do you understand?"

Chapter 18

"Frickin' boring" for Pittsburgh meant shipboard routine aboard Pittsburgh hadn't changed in four weeks. One advantage was watch station and submarine qualifications were going well for both officers and enlisted. The many lapsed administrative projects, which always slipped when you were in port and wanted to go home and see your family, were now almost all completed.

In the wardroom, Karen, Carla, John Walker, and several officers were getting ready to watch the president's speech to a group of students and academics at Georgetown University via a satellite feed coming into the ship's entertainment system.

The speech was part of the president building support for his "Peace in Our Time Initiative." As the president walked to the podium, he looked relaxed and well-focused. After all, he was addressing his people, the academics, the media and globalists. The congressmen and senators from all over country were critical of his policies, highly suspicious of North Korea and were unable to see past their many prejudices. As he approached the mike, the crowd stood and cheered. The president stood waving to his audience. When they finally sat down, he settled down to speak.

"Let me begin by saying I'm glad to have the opportunity to address this august group of international intellectuals who understand the changing face of diplomacy; people who understand that nationalism has no place in this new world. No longer can we live in a world where we do not respect our brother nations and their interests. It is not often one gets a chance to make a difference in the safety of the world, and Supreme Leader Kim Jong Un and I took a major step in moving to a real peace in our time."

The viewing was interrupted when the pantry door opened, and Seaman Ames entered. He saw the TV and pleadingly looked at Karen. "XO, ma'am, I need to set up for mid-rats."

Karen nodded and powered off the TV. "We can watch this on our tablets. It's recorded on the ship's system. We need to let the CSs set up."

As everybody started getting up, Karen commented. "I can't believe the president is foolish enough to think Kim Jong Un has any intention of carrying out this agreement other than taking the money."

John Walker didn't take the comment well. "Commander, you're wrong. I was with the president and the national security advisor when we negotiated the 'Peace in Our Time Initiative.' This is a great agreement with excellent support from both sides."

Karen scoffed. "That's what the pundits have said for the last two presidents when they attempted to do this, and all they got was egg on their faces."

John postured. "Well that may be true, but this president is different."

Karen laughed and shook her head.

John continued. "Furthermore, I'm not sure why we're spying off the coast of North Korea. That certainly wasn't in the mission directive I was shown."

Karen pulled up short as she opened the wardroom door, then turned and got right in John's face. "When did you see our mission directive? Your name wasn't on the distribution list."

John Walker knew he was caught in a difficult situation. "I was shown a copy when I received our orders to come to Pittsburgh."

Karen was now more concerned. "How did anyone have a copy to show you? That distribution list was closely held, and I don't remember seeing your organization on it."

John realized he screwed up. "Well, I don't know how. I just know I was shown the mission directive in our headquarters."

Karen was unhappy, but knew she was not going to solve this here. "Well, Mr. Walker, we're here because it's required by law and we were told to be here."

John refused to be cowered by her this time and looked her in the eye. "I think your captain's career is in jeopardy and that's why we're still here. We should have been out of here the moment that torpedo locked onto us."

Karen gave a threatening stare and John squirmed. "Mr. Walker, you are off base, and you will never mention something like that again. Do you understand?"

John Walker, knowing he had escaped with minor potential damage, nodded with trepidation.

Carla saw the tension and moved to calm things. "So, John, you were with the Korean negotiating team. Man, that must have been cool."

Karen got Carla's hint and backed off.

John was still upset but recovered. "Yes, it was. It was intense. The national security advisor, I think her name was Grains, was a fanatic. A 24-hour-a-day robot."

The other officers had left. Karen looked at Carla and John. "You two, let's get out of here."

As the three left the wardroom, John continued. "In fact, I got a call from her just before I came on board."

Karen heard this and turned back to John. "You mean, the national security adviser called you?"

"Why, yes, on the tug, just before I boarded."

Karen moved on but was concerned about John's comment. *Who all knew we were here?*

135

The UUVs had been sending their pictures back to Pittsburgh and when printed out they made an excellent collage of the continental shelf. Carla and John were looking over FT2 Smith's shoulders at the two laptop screens.

Drake, Karen, and the COB approached, and Drake looked at the maps. "Weps, what do have for us?"

Carla pointed to the map grid. "Sir, you wanted to know about repositioning. I think we can stay here another day. Then I recommend we move northeast to about here."

Karen had been looking the taped-together maps over, and pointed to an apparent line. "Weps, what's this line?"

Carla looked and shrugged. "I don't know."

Drake came in to take a look and tapped FT2 Smith on the shoulder. "Smith, can you go bring up this area and enlarge it for us on your screen?"

Smith made several keystrokes and mouse adjustments. The area around the line expanded on the laptop screen. "How is that?"

"Good, thank you." Drake took a closer look. "That looks like an old buried submarine communications cable. Smith, please zoom in further and move your cursor right and left."

As Smith did so, a small bare section of cable emerged.

Carla looked closely. "I've seen something like this when I worked at Special Projects." An excitement came over her. "That's exactly what that is! They had old cold war pictures like this in the special operations office at the DevRon."

Karen looked at the screen and asked, "Why in the world would the North Koreans be using an underwater communications cable?"

Drake moved over to the navigation chart where the

quartermaster was keeping track of Pittsburgh's position off the North Korean coast. Everyone followed.

"I don't know for sure, but geography would be one reason. In North Korea, with all the mountainous regions, land lines are tough, but a festooned underwater telecommunications cable bypasses all of that."

Karen looked puzzled. "You think the North Koreans might be using this?"

John Walker had just walked over and had observed the discussion. "Captain, that makes sense. We are getting no electronic communications and if the North Koreans think we are here they would be sending everything by hardwire cable."

Drake nodded. "Makes sense, but we have no way to check it."

A sly smile came over Carla's face. "That's not exactly true."

Drake looked at Carla. "How's that?"

"When we were told to shut down the DevRon's special project's programs, I sort of had one of the underwater modems shipped to me on the Pittsburgh, just in case."

"How in hell did you get away with that?" Drake paused a beat. "On second thought, don't tell me."

The COB had been quiet up to this point, but his wheels were turning. "Captain, we can use the SEAL delivery vehicle and install the modem. Easy launch, easy retrieval, compared to dropping off SEALs. I'm a qualified pilot and can take the lieutenant and her toy out there."

Karen was the first to respond, and she was not pleased. "Captain, we can't even think about hooking up some comms modem on that cable. We're already treading on legal thin ice, right on the very edge of North Korean waters."

Carla spoke up. "XO, we did this when I was at the DevRon."

Karen was irritated. "And the president shut that program down. This isn't the DevRon and that cable looks to be about five miles inside North Korean territorial waters. Any screw-up or accident puts the entire ship in danger, especially if we have to rescue someone."

Karen was frustrated. "My God, our decompression chamber is not sophisticated. I don't care how good Doc is, she has never handled a major decompression sickness problem at sea."

Drake was off in his own world, thinking. He looked at Karen. "XO, this is what we need to do." Not waiting for a reply, he spoke. "Weps, COB, let's do this."

Karen held her ground. "Captain, this looks like an act of desperation and well outside our orders."

At that moment John Walker spoke up. "Captain, I agree with the XO. We can't do that."

Drake was frustrated and got in John Walker's face. "Thank you for your thoughts, Mr. Walker, but you don't get a vote."

With his pride hurt, John shot back. "Sir, I was personally told by the president's national security advisor, Ms. Susan Grains, to stop you from carrying out any form of provocation to the North Koreans. I demand you not do this."

Drake laughed. "That's funny, I don't remember seeing her on my org chart." Drake thoughtfully looked around the control room, then to Carla and the COB. "Get on it."

Chapter 19

The next morning, the COB, Carla and two other crew members in scuba gear and wet suits brought the swimmer delivery vehicle out of its hanger. The COB carried the communications modem box and Carla carried what appeared to be a tool bag. They checked their underwater communications with Drake in Control.

As they got into the SDV, Drake cautioned them, "You two be careful. Don't worry about aborting if problems develop. We've still got lots of time."

Carla and the COB chuckled and looked at each other. "Yes, sir," they said in tandem. They departed Pittsburgh and transited toward the North Korean coast.

The SDV transited just below the surface. The sea was relatively calm; the June sea temperatures were warm. The transit to the selected cable installation site was uneventful. Over the headset, Carla heard Pittsburgh inform them they were right over the site. With that, the COB put the SDV into dive and down until they went to just above the ocean floor.

Carla could see the cable, and by looking along it as it stretched along the bottom, saw a good flat surface where the modem would easily fit. She pointed down. "COB, put her right over that area."

Once the SDV was steady, Carla got out first and swam to the cable. "COB, its bigger than I thought. We might have some issues."

The COB got out of the SDV. "Okay, whatever, but let's get this done fast." He lowered the modem down to Carla and she placed it on the cable. Carla was having some difficulty grabbing the right tool, but she finally found the right one and commenced the installation.

On Pittsburgh, Karen was on the scope and Drake was nervously pacing beside the conn. At that moment, the conn sonar speaker announced, "Conn, Sonar, picked up a new contact Sierra 234, bearing 302, drawing right. Sounds like a working trawler. Bottom bounce range 11,000 yards. Sending to fire control."

Karen rotated the scope to bearing 302. "Captain, I've got it. Trawler with a ninety-degree angle on the bow."

Drake did the math in his head and immediately understood the danger. "That put its track right over them." He picked up the underwater communications mike. "Weps, COB, get out of there. We've got a working trawler coming right at you."

The COB acknowledged Drake's warning. He had heard the trawler but now looked up and saw it in the distance coming right at them. "Lieutenant, we've got to get out of here."

Carla kept working. "I've just about got it." As the trawler closed, the noise was almost deafening.

Mike Riner rarely looked scared but now he was. "Weps, we've got to get out of here now!" He swam down to get Carla.

Just as he got there, Carla finished. "Got it."

The COB grabbed Carla and pulled her back and into the SDV. Before they could get out of the way, the trawler's drag nets went over them. The turbulence was so enormous that Carla got sucked out of the SDV. Tumbling in the turbulent water, her right swim fin got caught in the net. Unable to struggle free, Carla was pulled along with the trawler's nets.

In fear she called out, "COB get me out of here!"

The COB turned the SDV toward the trawler and put it at full throttle. The SDV had barely enough speed but was able to slowly close with the trawler's net. Carla was fighting to get loose, but her efforts had taken a toll. Her exhaustion was preventing her from breaking free. Finally, the COB saw her go limp and her mouthpiece fell out of her mouth. He left the SDV when it was just below Carla and drew his knife to cut Carla free of the swim fin that was holding her to the net.

As Carla's foot came out of the fin, she was tumbled downward toward the ocean floor. Just before she hit a rock outcropping, the COB got control of her and pulled her back to the SDV. He got her mouthpiece into her mouth and forced air into her lungs. Nothing happened for a few seconds until Carla started coughing. The cough forced the mouthpiece out of her mouth, and she regained consciousness.

The COB grabbed her like the daughter he never had, and put the mouthpiece back into her mouth. For what seem like hours, Carla attempted to get her breathing under control. Eventually, she looked over. "COB, where are we?"

The COB was relieved, and released Carla, putting her into the seat in the SDV. "We're going home."

On Pittsburgh, Drake and Karen were listening and heard what was happening.

"XO, get divers out there now!" Drake ordered. "And get Doc. We've got to be ready for them when they get back."

Karen acknowledged, "I'm worried about the bends; they've been down a long time." Karen quickly got to the operation middles level, right below the diver access hatch. The corpsman, HM1 Amanda Miller, was already dressed out and waiting.

Karen looked concerned and grabbed the access ladder and squeezed it hard to relieve her tension. She had been afraid something like this might happen and, other than Special Operations, no submarine had ever been put in this position.

141

Miller could tell she was worried. She had always been able to bring Karen out of her slumps. She put on her big smart-ass smile. "XO, I've got my gear, food and water already in the decompression chamber. I told you earlier I was hoping for some action but, come on, XO, this is a bit challenging."

Karen smiled and let go of the access ladder. "Okay, Miller, it's all up to you. Take care of Weps and the COB."

Miller started up the ladder. "I'm not worried about Lieutenant Kelly, but the COB – he's so old."

Miller's comment brought Karen back to ready. Miller always teased the COB about being the oldest guy on the ship. Karen smacked Miller on the rear end. "Make sure you bring them both back soon."

As the SDV approached Pittsburgh, three ship's divers met it and helped get Carla out of the vessel and into the decompression chamber. The COB entered right behind Carla, where Doc was waiting for them. Carla had several cuts and bruises. She was exhausted, and looked like a wet noodle. Doc shut the hatch and operated the valves to slowly drain the water out of the chamber and equalize.

When the water level dropped below Carla's face, Doc put an oxygen mask over the lieutenant's face. With her famous dry wit, she asked, "Hey, COB, welcome back. Did you and Weps have an exciting trip?"

Carla had known Doc Miller for only short time, but her humor was exactly what she needed to get past the fear that had almost overcome her.

Over the communication speaker, Drake called up. "Doc, how's it look?"

"Well, the COB is fine, old and ugly as ever, but Lieutenant Kelly needs a few stitches, a couple of cold compresses, and a good night's sleep. Other than that, we're good."

Drake had to laugh at Miller. She was another great find.

Eight hours later, the comms modem was linked to an onboard laptop. A bruised and bandaged Carla and Radioman Sanchez were manipulating the laptop keyboard keys.

Drake and the COB were talking quietly in the back of the conn. Drake was upset with himself and his head was down. He had sent Carla and the COB on a dangerous mission with serious consequences and almost lost both.

He looked up. "Jesus, COB, that was dumb. When you and Lt. Kelly struggled with that trawler, I realized I let my personal situation cloud my judgement."

The COB knew Drake Chandler better than anyone. "Captain, don't beat yourself up. It was a good call."

Drake gave the COB a questioning look. "Was it? Or was it desperation?" Drake put his hands over his face. "No, COB, I should have never sent you out to install that comms modem. That was one of the stupidest things I've done in my career."

The COB smiled, trying to comfort Drake. "Captain, you knew something was not right with this mission and you took a chance."

Drake was not consoled. "I know, but I'm supposed to take care of things like that so what almost happened to you wouldn't happen."

Karen and John Walker were observing Carla and Sanchez. The screen showed a series of presentations that carried some audio that was more like a screech than verbal communication. Carla looked into the notebook she had brought from the DevRon.

"Sanchez, we forgot to set up the HDMI interface with the

correct software."

Sanchez immediately pulled a cable out of the laptop and hit several software keys. She then reset the cable and immediately a clean screen came up. Carla selected the audio channels and immediately Korean was heard over the speaker.

John Walker moved closer and shook his head in amazement. "That's it. You've got it!"

A smile came over Drake's face as he looked at Carla. "Holy shit. It worked."

"Yes, sir, just like back at the DevRon."

John Walker knew he was now in a difficult situation. Was he going to engage in what he thought was wrong and in violation of what Susan Grains told him to do? He made his decision and looked at Drake. "I guess you'll want me to translate and make heads or tails of this."

Drake was concerned by his tone of voice. "Well, that's what we pay you for."

John countered, "I told you earlier what you are doing is illegal."

Carla put on her southern charm and moved next to John. "Come on, John, this is a huge opportunity to find out what's really happening."

John moved away from Carla and looked at Drake. "Captain, that is definitely not part of my mission and I have no intention of supporting this."

Drake was pissed as he sneered. "That would be our mission."

John gave him a sneer. "Our mission – my mission. It's my call, and I say no."

The COB moved into John Walker's face. "Listen, you little shit, you're not a Navy commander anymore. You're a goddamned contractor and riding my ship."

Before fisticuffs could start, Drake waved to the COB and Karen. "COB, back off. XO, COB, my stateroom."

John Walker knew he just caused a major problem for Drake Chandler and he was a little concerned. Chandler might have problems with his current ComSubRon 15 commander, but based on what happened to a former assistant secretary of the Navy, Chandler knew how to play hard-ball politics. He turned and left Control and went back to his stateroom.

Drake knew that sometime during the mission, John Walker was going to be a problem. He was just unhappy it had to be now. They really needed his and his team's expertise. As he, Karen and the COB entered his stateroom he knew he first had to calm the COB down. He was pissed, and flames were coming out of his ears.

"Pardon my French, sir, but this is fucking bullshit! I'm going to kill that little bastard. He doesn't have the right to challenge your authority."

As the COB talked, some of the emotion started to wear off. Drake knew that in many ways, Walker was right. "COB, our mission has several aspects and unfortunately Walker is a key element in the most important of those. We probably need to suck it up and come up with a work-around."

Karen had been thinking about this as the interaction in Control unfolded and tried to inject herself, but Drake waved her off. "I know you're upset, but we're working well outside our current guidance and directions."

The COB was having nothing of this. "Why don't I have a one-on-one counseling with the little shit."

Drake smiled and chuckled, breaking the tension. "As much as I would like that, we can't do it."

Karen finally saw a chance to get a word in. "I think we can help this out by moving the modem laptop into Radio right next to Walker's spook team consoles. I'm not comfortable with what we're doing now and having it in Control lets everybody on board see it. I certainly don't want the entire crew to know what's going on." She smirked and laughed. "Although, they probably already know."

Drake laughed with Karen. Karen continued, "I agree. Walker's bored. Once it's in Radio, with a bit of Lt. Kelly's help, I think Walker will more than likely start playing with it. In the meantime, let's download a Korean translation app. Maybe our using a work-around without them will generate some jealousy."

Karen was still concerned. "You know, Captain, I don't like this. Walker was involved in the North Korean negotiation team and somehow, he gets dropped into Pittsburgh as leader of the spook team and then we get attacked."

The COB looked at her. "Are you saying he may be a spy?"

Karen paused. "Maybe. He got a phone call from the national security advisor just before he got onboard, and that doesn't seem kosher."

Drake thought about his. "I don't think so." He took a thoughtful pause. "Walker seems to like Chief Belt. Why don't you see if she can use her female charms to help get Mr. Walker to come around?"

Karen smiled and shook her head. "First Kelly and then Belt – the old one-two. That's awfully sexist, but I get the gist of what you mean."

Chapter 20

Moving the modem processer laptops to Radio went better than expected. Carla had softened up John Walker and Chief Belt used her ample leadership and schmoozing skills to get him involved. The downloading and use of the Korean translation app had grated on the pride of the spook team and they stared showing an interest. The tension with Walker had subsided a bit. The communications traffic moving through the underwater cable was significant. No doubt the North Koreans were routing most of their traffic that way.

Karen was working in her stateroom right after evening meal. The was a knock on her door and YNC Tubbs entered. Tubbs had been with Drake Chandler when he was an XO. He had gone off to a tour in Washington D.C., where he quickly learned he didn't belong in that environment. He asked to leave the crazy puzzle palace early to come to Guam to be with his old XO.

Tubbs was a rough around the edges, but a better leading yeoman was not to be found. The junior officers were all initially afraid of him. They would ask him for something, and he would give them a ration of crap for not knowing how to do their jobs, while he deftly found what they needed and typed it up for them as he bitched. It just took about three interactions and the JOs finally figured it out.

Karen asked him, "What's up?"

Tubbs shut the stateroom door and put a folder on Karen's desk. "Sir, it's this Seaman Ames. His record just doesn't make sense. It's got nothing in it."

Karen shrugged. "Okay. Why do we care?"

As Karen picked up the folder and perused it, Tubbs

looked over her shoulder. "He reenlisted after being out of the Navy for only a year, but he doesn't have the paper trail that you'd expect. Nothing about prior schools, bootcamp or CS 'A' school."

Karen nodded. "Okay, we'll look at that when we get back into port."

Tubbs was concerned. "There's something else."

Karen looked up at Tubbs.

"For never having been on a submarine, he knows his way around too well."

"So, what are you trying to say?"

Tubbs was a little concerned about what he was going to convey. "I'm trying to say I don't trust the guy."

After lunch, Drake decided to go up to Radio and read the latest traffic. He had observed the integration of the comms modem laptop into Radio and was proud of his crew. They knew of the tension but worked with the spook team to start copying and analyzing all the traffic. On entry, Drake saw John Walker observing the comms modem laptop.

"John, I want to thank you and your team for working with us on the traffic coming through the comms modem. I'll make sure that if there is any problem, I will not let it blow back on you."

John was surprised, after his rather abusive interaction with Drake Chandler, that he would say something like that. "Well, thank you, sir. We saw your team working hard to do something we do for a living, and I told them that we will support you all we can. Also, Chief Belt was quite persuasive." John gave Drake a thankful look. "And to tell you the truth, at least now we have something to do. Now I think we know why there has been so little electronic communications. These last several days have been busy and given us a chance to do what we do best."

Drake was relieved that he had overcome a potential problem. He looked at John. "This stuff comes across as gibberish to me even when I read it in English."

John gave Drake a sort of look of condescension. "It's not gibberish to me, and then that's why I'm the spook team leader."

Drake took back his last good thought of Walker and now wanted to kick him in the teeth, but he sucked it up. "Yeah, right!"

At that moment, a new translated message came across the laptop processor. John's face immediately became concerned and he looked at Drake and stuttered. "Aha...aha...aha, Captain, something's wrong. I think the North Koreans may be launching a nuclear strike disguised as a missile test."

Drake was perplexed and moved next to John. "They what?"

John pointed to a message. "Yes, sir. All week I have been reading about some upcoming missile test, but just now there was a reference to that test as the American Goryeon."

Drake was confused. "The what?"

John could tell Drake didn't understand. "The Goryeon Dynasty was a period when the greatest Korean Warlords destroyed all of their enemies. In recent political writings, the North Koreans refer to their dominance of the world as their Goryeon heritage."

Drake was now totally in the dark. "Okay. So, what does that mean to me?"

"What it means is I think the North Koreans are planning a nuclear weapon launch at the United States."

Drake retorted. "Don't give me that. Intelligence states they have not progressed to that point yet."

John was concerned. Drake could see it in his face.

149

John continued, "Neither did our experts during our 'Peace in Our Time' negotiations."

Now Drake was alarmed. "What are you trying to say?"

John was uncomfortable, but he confessed. "For the past week there have been several message anomalies concerning nuclear weapons and missile tests coming in."

Now Drake was upset. "And you didn't tell anyone?"

John defensively said, "I just disregarded them because they made no sense. Then this message makes it look like there's going to be a nuclear attack."

Now Drake was pissed. Really pissed. "And you didn't tell me!"

This hit a nerve in John. "Listen, Captain, I do my job and I don't need a bunch of arrogant fucking bubbleheads telling me what to do."

Drake stepped over to the announcing system mike and picked it up. "XO, Chief of the boat, lay to Radio."

Throughout the ship the crew looked at one another. They heard the fear in the skipper's voice. In the next two minutes, the COB followed by the XO entered Radio. Drake motioned them over the comms modem laptop. "XO, COB, we have a huge problem. We need to get a message out ASAP."

Being on station twelve miles off the North Korean coast, Pittsburgh again had to use the Submarine Special Communication System. Its low-frequency random noise carrier frequency took four hours transmit the message and, once received, about thirty minutes to make the ComSubLant, Pentagon and White House aware that something critical just came in. A big downside for Drake was it didn't go to his immediate commanders with ComSubGruSeven or ComSubPac.

Michelle Pak received the call from the NSA saying they had a critical message that could only be hand delivered to the president, secretary of defense, and the president's NSA. The security personnel knew Michelle had all the needed security credentials. She ordered a car, went to Fort Meade, and personally receipted for the messages and brought them back to the White House.

Susan was in her office drafting up a new speech for the president to give at his upcoming Fourth of July meetings at Stanford and the University of California, Berkley, when Michelle knocked and entered.

"Ma'am, I just got this SSCS message from the NSA at Fort Meade. One for you, one for State and one for Defense."

Susan shook her head in frustration. "This no doubt must be from the fucking Chandler."

Michelle nodded.

As Susan opened and read the cryptic message, she couldn't believe what she was reading. She fully understood that her failure to get the submarine off the coast of North Korea was coming back to haunt her. She thought to herself, what does some desperate loser commander on a fucking submarine off the coast of North Korea understand about international diplomacy?

"Michelle, I want the chief of staff, Defense and SecNav and the CNO in the Situation Room at four p.m., and bring Rentner in on video conference. Make sure they have seen this before the meeting."

Clark James, Tom Reynolds, Judith Wilson, and Admiral Gensen had all arrived early and had read the message. Now they were trying to figure out how the NSA would react. On arrival, Michelle had given them copies of the Pittsburgh message they had not seen.

Judith Wilson shook her head. "Admiral, your boy Chandler certainly know how to stir up a hornet's nest."

Admiral Gensen was quietly shaking his head as he read the message.

Susan entered the room. She was not a happy camper. Her normal perfectly fitting clothes, hair and makeup were disheveled, and it was obvious she wanted to take scalps.

"This fucking submarine commander, who is in the process of getting fired, sends off a message like this! Jesus Christ, this could cause an international incident."

Susan dropped into the chair at the head of the table and mockingly blurted out. "'The North Koreans may be preparing a nuclear launch against the United States.' Ridiculous!"

Clark James was the first to try and get a word in. "I agree."

Susan lashed out again. "I told you I didn't want that submarine out there and now look what has happened."

Admiral Gensen had finished his contemplation. "Director, we pulled our ABM ships off the coast of North Korea, but I think we might want to move one of them back."

Susan was ready for this. "Admiral, you're a bigger fool than I thought you were. We're talking about the president's major diplomatic triumph and the removal of a major threat of nuclear war to the world." She threateningly looked at each of them in the room. "Your expertise is evidently moving little warships around the world. Mine is making sure the world is safe and no longer threatened by a nuclear armed madman."

Susan saw she had taken away any thought of challenging her. She was good at that.

Clark James spoke up in support. "Our satellite images of the missile launch areas show nothing out of the ordinary. We would have seen something if they were preparing a nuclear weapon."

Tom Reynolds shook his head. "Yes, Clark, but there's been a lot of new building in those areas. They could have easily hidden those efforts."

Finally, Admiral Rentner chimed in from video link. The admiral was a political player and had worked with Susan on many fronts. "I share the director's concern. Drake Chandler is under extreme pressure, having had a falling out with his commodore. If there had not been the problem with the Illinois, we would have had Tom Witson up there and this would not be an issue."

Vice Admiral Renter's input moved the discussion into Susan's court, and she took advantage. "So, we get this guy and his submarine out of there."

Clark James provided the answer. "As much as this is an irritation, his communications are only coming to us. We still have a big problem with Congress and parts of the Pentagon that Tom and Admiral Gensen can't get under control. I think we let him be and not stir up a hornet's nest."

Susan was furious. "You've got to be kidding me! I'm going to the president."

Clark shook his head. "Oh, yeah, and tell him about this. That will be on the front page of every paper and the lead story on all newscasts for the next two weeks. No, Susan. We let this slide."

The meeting broke up and, still pissed, Susan returned to her office. She couldn't concentrate. She buzzed Michelle. "Michelle, get me Jong on the secure phone."

Michelle entered Susan's office and took a security key and put it into her secure phone. It took about two minutes keying, but she had Jong on the line. Michelle left, shutting the door behind her.

Jong came on the phone and was met with Susan's direct challenge. "Mr. Song, what is going on?"

Jong was not used to a woman challenging him like that, but he sucked it up. "What do you mean, Madam National Security Advisor?"

"Well, our submarine off your coast reported they intercepted a communication that you may be launching a nuclear weapon at the United States, disguised as a missile test."

Jong raised his eyebrows in surprise at how that could have gotten to Washington. Feigning concern and irritation, he responded. "Susan, how can you even think that of us? We're not crazy. I cannot believe you even thought that might be true."

Jong could sense Susan was still concerned, as she responded, "Okay. But our military is aware of the submarine's message and, even though I know it's not true, they have considerable clout here in Washington."

Jong had to get this under control and knew how to do it. "Well, I can assure you our supreme leader looks at this agreement with your president as a capstone of his reign. I can't even imagine my mentioning your suspicion. I can guarantee you he would renounce it and might renounce the entire 'Peace in Our Time Initiative.'"

Susan bit her lower lip. "I figured that, but I needed you to know."

Jong had escaped. Smiling, he responded, "Thank you. I will immediately find out if someone in my organization was behind this preposterous lie. Let's stay in touch, so things like this don't derail our efforts."

Susan felt much better. "Thank you."

Jong was concerned as he got his people into the conference room in the early afternoon. As he walked across the Tonghae Satellite Launching Ground, he observed the intricately choreographed ballet of carts and trucks innocently moving easily visible nondescript items and equipment. This let the U.S. satellites have something to report, while hidden in the dance were the key parts to the nuclear weapon in the final stages for launch at the United States.

In the conference room, Jong's staff were quietly drinking tea and looking out over the launch ground. As Jong entered, immediate quiet come over the room. The staff was on edge. The look on Jong's face was harsher than normal and they didn't like last minutes meetings like this – people died.

Jong started. "Well, gentlemen, you have screwed up again. My American friend tells me this submarine off our coast found out about our plan."

The impact on everyone was immediate. There was concern.

General Yun Lyun spoke up. "But, sir, there is no way a submarine could have done that. We stopped all traffic by unsecure means two months ago."

Jong scowled. "Then, so much for your secure traffic. You need to find out how that happened."

The operations manager, Kim Shin-Jo spoke up. "It may be just too late for the Americans and that submarine. We have completed mating our nuclear warhead to our Taeppodong-2 Goryeon missile."

Jong knew this, but hearing Shin-Jo validate his information comforted him. "That's good, but we need to press

155

ahead and make sure our special surprise for the American president goes on as scheduled. And you, Admiral Ryu, need to destroy that submarine."

Admiral Ryu, who thought he had hidden well enough behind the other staff members not to be seen, now emerged. "Yes, sir, but this Commander Chandler, I fear, is dangerous. He didn't respond to our attack like you told us and he evidently has a history of not following orders."

Song moved in front of the Admiral and sneered. "Admiral, you were supposed to take care of him. I should be getting another location beacon from the submarine soon and you need to be ready."

Jong put on his most harsh expression. "And this time, Admiral, don't fail me!"

PART FOUR – NUCLEAR ATTACK

Chapter 21

Drake was surprised he had not received a response from the rather forceful message he had sent. It still bothered him that his immediate commanders, Captain East and Admiral Collar, might not be seeing them. They would have at least sent something to let him know they were received and would have provided some guidance without the political bullshit that surrounds a Pentagon response.

John Walker was in Radio, having decided to skip lunch. They always played cribbage. He just wasn't into that and he disliked not winning. He heard the sound on the comms modem laptop indicating new traffic and strolled over behind Chief Belt. As he translated the message, he became concerned. He asked Chief Belt to print out the last traffic and asked where the Captain and Exec were.

Rita Belt could tell something was seriously wrong by the expression on John's face. "I'm sure they're in the wardroom, finishing lunch."

With a quick thank you, he hustled out of Radio with his copies. As he left, Chief Belt picked up the phone and called the chief's quarters. The COB picked up. "COB, something big is going down. You need to get to the wardroom now."

As the COB opened the chief's quarters door, John Walker hurried past. The COB saw his expression and hurried to fall in behind him. "Where you headed so fast Mr. Walker?"

John said nothing but proceeded on.

157

In the wardroom, Drake and Karen were playing cribbage while everyone else watched. Karen played her hand and pegged. "That would be 15-2, 15-4, 15-6 and 8, and I am out."

Exasperated, Drake shrugged. "XO, you're a goddamn machine."

Karen smiled as Carla shook her head. "Captain, you always say that. You ever think maybe you're not that good?"

Karen picked up the cards and pegs. "Weps, you're next."

As Carla moved the cribbage board toward her, the wardroom door opened, and John Walker entered with the COB right behind him.

Drake smiled when they entered. "John, come to participate in a little cribbage?"

John rolled his eyes. "No, sir, I don't do cribbage. But here is something you need to see."

John handed Drake, Karen, and Carla copies of the message he had translated and printed out, and let them read.

Karen was the first to pick up the essence. "My God, they've mated a nuclear weapon on a Taepodong-2 missile. That's got the range to hit the west coast of the U.S."

Carla recognized an even more sinister point. "Christ, they're going to launch on the Fourth of July, so it goes off over San Francisco at 2100 local time."

The COB spoke up. "Everyone will be outside watching fireworks and they'll see their deaths coming."

Carla looked down in fear and rage. "Depending on what elevation they set, it could kill millions of people with the direct effects."

Everyone in the wardroom except Drake and Karen had broken into conversation. Drake had feared this and had already been talking with Karen, putting scenarios together in their minds.

The timing was interesting – maximum impact.

"They need to get those BMD cruisers and destroyers back on station," Drake said.

Carla countered, "And if they don't?"

Drake had worried about this. "We have to make them believe."

Karen had completed her back-of-the-envelope calculations in her head. "If my geography and math are right, that means 1230 p.m. local launch two days from now, from the Tonghae Satellite Launching Ground."

Drake stood up, went to the wall, and set the countdown clock they used for drills and training sessions for 1230 p.m. in two days. "We have to find a solution fast. We've got two days."

The wardroom 27 MC speaker clicked on. The OOD shouted over the electronic screech in the background, "Captain, officer of the deck, just after we blew sanitaries we picked up that loud electronic screeching in the ESM receiver."

The COB moved next to Drake. "Sir, we definitely have a spy on board."

Drake looked at Karen. "XO, get up into radio and start drafting a message to the world about what we've discovered. We'll still need to send this using the SSC, so Admiral Collar at ComSubPac and Commodore Mains at ComSubGruSeven will have no idea what's going on. We need some horsepower if we expect to get some intelligent guidance. "

Karen looked concerned. "Sir, that will pinpoint our location."

Drake chuckled and put his arms out. "It's not like the North Koreans don't know where we are right now." He turned to the navigator, who was reviewing logs. "Nav, get up into control and relocate us four miles inside the twelve-mile limit."

This caused Karen to wince. "But, sir, we can't do that. It's in direct violation of our orders and Commodore East's direct warning."

Drake nodded. "XO, right, but right now we are at something slightly short of war. We need to do whatever it takes to make sure that war never starts." Drake smirked. "And besides, what a perfect place to hide."

Thirty minutes later, Drake entered Radio. Karen had just finished her draft of the message. "What ya' got?" queried Drake, as he came in behind her and looked over her shoulder.

FROM: USS PITTSBURGH

SUBJ: Update on North Korean Nuclear Attack on United States

1. (TS) USS Pittsburgh in receipt of recent message stating North Koreans mated a nuclear weapon on a Taepodong-2 missile

2. (TS) Target of nuclear attack will be San Francisco at 2100 local on 4 July.

3. (TS) USS Pittsburgh strongly recommends relocating ABM ships back off the coast of North Korea ASAP.

4. (TS) Indication of spy on board. Locator beacon was recently released from ship – looking for him now.

Drake squinted, then smiled. "XO, you like to keep it straight forward and direct. Drop the fourth line. They don't need to know that." He turned to the communicator, Mike Conklin. "Com, get this sent via the EHF Special Communication Circuit."

Mike nodded "Yes, sir."

Drake picked up the Radio 27 MC handset. "Officer of the deck: rig ship for ultra quiet."

Chapter 22

Susan had been at other meetings when Michele had pulled her away to come back to the office. Something big was up because she had seen calls and texts from the chief of staff, Admiral Rentner and the Pentagon during her sessions. Something was up.

Michele gave Susan a copy of the Pittsburgh message. As she read it, her frustration built and it finally got the best of her. She threw her coffee cup and yelled at Michele. "Why didn't I see this earlier and, my God, who all was this sent to?"

Now her opponents had more time to prepare and maybe more ammunition to take action that she knew might seriously threaten the president's initiative. A meeting was set up for one hour from now and Susan hit the phones to find allies to support her position.

An hour later, the key personnel and a covey of others were sitting around the conference table in the Situation Room. Their aides all sat back against the wall. Way too many people were involved for Susan's taste, but with the content of Pittsburgh's message, she had to put up with it. Michele entered and powered up the conferencing video monitor. So now, the operational commanders, ComSubPac and ComSubGruSeven, had been brought in on the discussion. Just what she didn't need.

Susan decided to go on the attack. "I told you all earlier this Chandler guy was a nutcase. I have heard from his direct commander, Commodore Stephan Sails, and from Admiral Rentner, the head of the submarine force. So, Tom, what are we supposed to do with this most recent message. His allegations are preposterous."

Immediately the chief of staff supported Susan. "Tom, we

161

had this discussion several weeks ago and you have done nothing."

The CNO stepped in. "Preposterous or not, I'm having real concerns about our ballistic missile defense ships not being on the coast of North Korea."

Susan fired back. "My God, this Chandler is a deranged man who should never have been sent on this mission."

The secretary of defense jumped in. "The BDM ships are close. We have them there to monitor the upcoming missile testing."

Susan went back on the attack. "So, Admiral, are you are ready to be singled out as the individual who scuttled the 'Peace in Our Time' initiative? You're the one who will be responsible for any use of nuclear weapons in the future." Susan glowered while looking around at all at the table and on the video monitors. Pointing at each of them she said, "And that goes for all of you."

Susan's comment stymied any challenges. The people around the conference table and those coming in on video conference took stock of what the national security advisor was saying, and clammed up.

CIA Director Michael Ardor spoke up in support of Susan. "I have been talking with the National Reconnaissance Office and they are seeing no activity at the Tonghae Launching area other than actions that are related to the upcoming missile tests. Certainly nothing that looks like preparation for a nuclear launch."

Now Susan was impassioned as she stood. "Ladies and gentlemen, we have all the facts. We need to ignore this one man's ridiculous allegation."

At that point Admiral Collar stepped into the fray. "Madam Director, I was the one who sent Drake Chandler on that mission. He and his ship have special skills. I know he would not have sent that message without good cause."

Susan needed to beat down this last challenge. "So, Admiral, you are another culprit who should be relieved of your command. You obviously don't understand international diplomacy and certainly don't understand the president's strong belief that this initiative is critical to the safety of the world."

Having taken his beat-down, Admiral Collar asked the last question. "Has anyone told the president?"

This question infuriated Susan, and she changed the subject. "It is settled. We're getting this submarine away from the North Korean coast."

The meeting broke up, and Michele picked up all the messages and shredded them as she always did and returned to her office to pick up her satellite phone.

Four hours later, Drake looked at the incoming message. He had been surprised he didn't get a quicker response from ComSubPac, but this message came from Vice Admiral Rentner's shop at Commander Submarine Force in Norfolk, Virginia. Carla read it aloud as they looked at it.

FROM: COMSUBFOR
To: USS PITTSBURGH
SUBJ: Mission Complete
1. (S) USS Pittsburgh mission complete
2. (S) Stop all electronic monitoring
3. (S) USS Pittsburgh depart North Korean waters via tracks to be provided.

Carla chuckled. "A bit short."

Karen looked at Drake and adamantly chimed in. "But to the point."

Drake slowly read the message again. "It doesn't make sense. Do they think we're making this up?"

Karen was not sure how to take that comment. "Sir, it's straight forward. We have no choice. We need to clear the area."

John Walker moved next to Karen. "Captain, I understand my position." He raised his hands as if they were quotation marks. "I know I don't have a vote, but I do understand the National Command Authority is telling us to leave. We are in the middle of the president's historical foreign policy legacy and they no doubt have intelligence discounting our allegations."

Drake took in John's comment. "This has nothing to do with presidential legacies. We're talking about nuclear war and the safety and security of the United States."

Karen stiffened. "But, Captain, this is a direct order."

Carla challenged Karen. "XO, this is the captain's ship. What he says, goes."

Karen confronted Carla. "This is a legal order."

The COB had been listening to this discussion and was now pissed at Karen. "Legal – illegal. That's all bullshit when you know a country is going to attack the United States."

Chief Belt brought over a printout of a new message that had just been intercepted. Drake raised his hand to quiet everybody. Drake and Karen read the message with alarm.

Drake said, "Interesting. Not only do the North Koreans know we intercepted their nuclear launch plans, but they also know my name, the ship's name and our supposed location."

Karen was now having a change of heart. "How did they get those details"

Drake responded, "I don't know, but it has danger written all over it." Drake stood back and thought a minute. "We're going to send a much more direct message and lay out exactly what I intend to do."

Over the Radio 27 MC speaker the OOD called. "Captain, office of the deck, Sonar requests your presence."

Drake, Karen, and the COB entered Sonar and started looking at the displays. The sonar supervisor pointed to a series of lines on a display. "Captain, about thirty minutes ago we picked up what I now think is a large group of warships. There is at least one Najin-class frigate and several Sariwon-class corvettes, all very ASW capable."

Karen did the geometry in her head. "Those traces are on the bearing to the North Korean naval base at Wonsan."

There was a brightening of all the lines on the screen, followed by a display operator calling out, "Supervisor, I just heard an active sonar I think corresponds to a SID-3 sonar pulse. If my memory serves me right, that is a very capable active sonar."

A look of concern came over Drake.

The COB spoke up. "Yes, it's a very capable sonar, but *having* a capable sonar and knowing how to use it are two different things."

Drake looked at Karen. "Agree, COB, but I'm glad we're well away from our earlier position."

Back in Radio, Drake, Karen, the communicator, Mike Conklin, and John Walker looked at the message Drake had prepared. Karen read it aloud.

FROM: USS PITTSBURGH

SUBJ: FOLLOW UP

1. (S) In receipt of mission termination message.

2. (TS) Pittsburgh strongly recommends continuing mission.

3. (TS) Nuclear attack planned for Northern California on the 4th of July at 2100 local.

4. (TS) Pittsburgh recommends BMD ships reposition immediately.

5. (TS) Separate topics:

A. (TS) Recent intercept indicates North Korea aware of US concerns about nuclear attack and the name and location of USS Pittsburgh and its Commanding Officer.

B. (TS) With no Ballistic Missile Defense or other platforms for monitoring available, USS Pittsburgh intends to maintain current position and mission status until further guidance.

As she listened to the message, Karen was troubled. "Captain, you realize this is a career breaker no matter what happens."

Drake always appreciated his exec's honesty. "Yeah, I do, but there's the potential start of a nuclear war if we don't."

John challenged Drake. "We don't know that for sure. The National Command Authority may have intelligence that makes this irrelevant."

Drake thought about John's comment. "That is true, but they certainly have not been forthcoming with any background." Finally, Drake tuned to the communicator. "Tom, send it."

At that moment three very loud active sonar transmissions were heard thought the hull. Drake looked at Karen. "Let's see what our North Korean friends have in store for us."

Chapter 23

Captain Sung Park was happy to be at sea, away from ignorant eyes and the disdain of superiors who had no idea what life was like at sea, and even less what it was like to conduct ASW. After his failure over a month ago to get the U.S. submarine, he now feared for his life. His mentor, if that's what you would call him, Admiral Ryu, would throw him to the wolves if it meant saving his hide, and right now, he feared that possibility. At least this time he had a much larger flotilla of ships, including three of the new Najin-class light frigates and two Sariwon-class corvettes with the latest sonars.

He also had some surprises for this Commander Drake Chandler who had successfully slipped through Mr. Song's supposedly tight net. Song was a fool, but a powerful one. Just because he provided a location doesn't mean you can find and sink an America submarine. This Chandler was undoubtedly better than the average submarine captain.

His second-in-command came to the bridge and informed him the conference video with Admiral Ryu and Mr. Song was ready. In the tight ship's operations center a video monitor was set up in a conference room, and the Admiral and Mr. Song were just arriving at their location. After routine greeting protocols, Admiral Ryu asked, "Captain Sung Park, are you on station and are your ships in position?"

Sung Park fought the urge to be sarcastic. Ryu had never commanded at sea or operated in a combined naval operation. He was a relative of the supreme leader. "Yes, sir. Our ships are in the exact location that you and Mr. Song directed. Active sonar search and airborne dipping and sonobuoy searches are in progress."

Jong didn't trust the navy, especially after the last fiasco. He especially didn't trust Admiral Ryu, whose father was an admiral., Ryu spent most of his time sucking up to his senior officers, including Jong. He was sure the admiral's interference in their first effort to sink Pittsburgh caused the failure.

Captain Park, on the other hand, was an at-sea operator, which was much more satisfying to Jong. Park's major weakness was he had no vision or cleverness to make him comfortable that all avenues of execution had been taken.

Jong asked, "Captain Park, tell me you know what you are doing."

A bit insulted, Sung Park retorted, "Yes, sir, I know what I am doing, and I thank you for providing the right assets for this effort."

Admiral Ryu felt Park's remark was really a jab at him. "Mister Song, are you sure you can trust your American friend?"

Song gave the admiral a raised eyebrow, thinking maybe the old fart was a little combative. "Well, Admiral, she has certainly been more accurate than you."

That comment deflated Ryu and the expression on his face hardened.

On Pittsburgh, it had been noisy for the last twelve hours. Pittsburgh moved four miles inside the North Korean twelve-mile territorial limit, leaving the ASW search five to six miles to the east of them. The constant active sonar search was definitely more professional than the last one, but the constant spikes of noise made sleeping difficult.

In the wardroom, Drake, Karen, Carla, and most of the officers were finishing lunch. Karen, in her typical looking-for-a-victim voice, asked "Is anyone a up for cribbage?"

Carla responded, "Not me. Those active sonar transmissions make my skin crawl. They just need to stop."

Karen laughed. "Come on Weps, I haven't trounced you in a while."

Drake watched this little interaction with amusement. "Well, the North Koreans are doing their best and no doubt are confused that they can't find us."

There was a knock on the door, and the COB entered and moved between Drake and Karen. Karen saw a chance for new blood. "Well, COB, you're late for dessert but maybe we can interest you in a game of cribbage."

"Well, ma'am, I've heard about your prowess and I don't think I'm ready to get trashed."

The wardroom members laughed, and Drake asked, "What's up?"

The COB responded, "Sir, we have new problem. There are some rumblings among the crew that we are operating in direct violations of our orders."

Drake chuckled. "Well, I guess we should give them some credit. Since we haven't had a response to our last message, they're exactly right. Any thoughts?"

The COB looked concerned. "Well, sir, there's a small band of the usual agitators, but I'm pretty sure that Mr. Walker's team is behind this. I think you need to address the crew and lay out what's going on."

Drake looked around the wardroom and thought to himself, then said, "You're right. Let's set something up in the mess decks after evening meal. XO, put a chart together to help me show what we're doing."

After evening meal, the mess deck was full of Pittsburgh sailors. Karen had posted a chart on the back wall showing the

North Korean coast, the Tonghae Satellite Launching Ground, the position of the North Korea ASW operation and Pittsburgh's location. The crew knew about the threat of a North Korean nuclear attack on the United States, but they were surprised when they saw their position inside the twelve-mile limit.

Drake entered. The crew started to stand but Drake waved for them to stay seated. As he reached the front of the group he looked back at the chart.

"I want to thank you all for taking time out of your few free hours to come and listen to want we're doing. Much of what I am about to tell you is at a security level that only I and the XO are cleared for, but I think you need to understand what we are doing."

At that moment, one of the spook team members, Petty Office Teacher, called out, "Captain, we are concerned that our safety is in jeopardy because you want to make a name for yourself and have put us in danger."

The surrounding Pittsburgh crewmembers started to boo and told him to shut the fuck up.

The COB stepped forward to take charge, but Drake waved him back and quieted down the crew. "Well, Petty Officer Teacher, this is a warship. One of our jobs is to step up and prevent enemies of the United States from attacking our country or putting it in danger."

Drake's comment was met with a chorus of negative comments directed at Teacher.

Doc stood and gave Petty Officer Teacher a harsh look. "Teacher, why are you here? You're not even a Pittsburgh crew member."

Drake let the comments die down. "As Petty Office Teacher well knows, we have learned the North Koreans intend to launch a nuclear missile at the United States on the Fourth of July."

Teacher felt the peer pressure and tried to defend himself. "Then, sir, why haven't the president and the military done something? They did order us to depart the area."

This comment quieted the crew and they looked questioningly among themselves.

The COB stepped in. "Gentlemen and ladies, I assure you, they are aware."

Drake wasn't happy the COB had barged in. "Right now, we may well be the only thing between the United States and a nuclear war. We have all sworn to give our lives to protect our country and we're not going to let North Korea attack the United States on our watch."

That comment struck the right tone in the heart of the crew. They knew exactly what he was talking about. A renewed sense of concern, pride and patriotism showed on their faces.

Drake finished his remarks by commenting, "Things may get dangerous in the next few days. We've trained over and over for these types of situations, but tomorrow they may become real. It's not like going to the fire or flooding trainer, where, if things go wrong, the instructors put out the fire or stop the flooding. It will be real."

With that, Drake, the COB and Karen left. The crew just sat there and didn't move or talk with one another. They were proud Pittsburgh sailors. They knew what was coming. They felt confident that their captain would do the right things to keep them safe.

Chapter 24

The next morning, Drake sat in his chair on the conn. Carla was the OOD and Karen was observing the geo plot. The active sonar pings had not let up throughout the night. Bottom-bounce ranges and multiple bearing lines still showed the ASW activity to be six miles to the east. No doubt, they were still searching the area from where the locator beacon had emerged from Pittsburgh.

Drake moved over to the plot. "XO, put your hands around where you think the ASW flotilla is located."

Karen looked puzzled as she cupped her hands around a four-inch circle where the bearing lines generally crossed and estimated ranges were shown. Karen looked at Drake. "What are you thinking?"

Drake looked at the plot coordinator. "Give me a range and bearing to the center of the circle the XO just showed us."

Lieutenant Tom Dawson swung the sliding protractor arm and placed on a line between Pittsburgh and the center of the circle. "Sir, bearing zero-eight-eight range, 13,500 yards."

Drake nodded. "Thank you." Turning to Karen, he said, "XO, generate a surface target Master Four for me on that range and bearing. Have the weapons control panel operator set the torpedo in Tube Two for surface mode, shallow medium to low speed transit, and circular search mode."

Karen, walking to the weapons control panels, smiled. "A good just-in-case." She observed Lieutenant Pott enter the solution and Petty Officer Smith adjust settings for the weapons. With all torpedo tube outer doors open, this weapon was ready for immediate launch. Karen called out "Solution ready, Master Four;

172

weapon ready, Master Four."

Carla was observing the UUV laptop displays. "Captain, here's something odd."

Drake got up and moved next to Carla. Carla pointed to the display. "These swirls of sand and debris. It's like something is disturbing the bottom behind us."

Drake peered in for a closer look. "Whatever is causing that disturbance would have to be pretty big." Drake paused a beat. "I wonder if we have a friend back there?" He nodded to Carla and they moved to Sonar.

As they entered, the supervisor acknowledged their arrival with a nod. "Yes, sir?"

"Supervisor, shift analysis and classification to the toward array endfire and look for a diesel submarine."

The supervisor was confused. "A diesel submarine?"

"Yes, a diesel sub."

The middle console operator modified his screen and soon the endfire beams were updating with new lines. As they built, there were several discontinuities. The operator focused on those points. "Supervisor, I am starting to see motor slot lines in the endfire. They align to a North Korean Sang-O class diesel submarine."

Drake nodded. "And he's close."

Twelve hundred yards behind Pittsburgh, the North Korean Sang-O-class submarine, Sagot, was conducting ASW searches looking for the U.S. submarine. Sagot was well inside the twelve-miles limit by order of Captain Park. The commanding officer, Sojwa Ji Kim stood in his attack center and observed his operators. He felt he should have been out with the main ASW forces. The submarine's attack center was very small and crowded and manned for battle stations.

His XO put his hand over the ear piece on his headset. "Captain, Sonar reports possible U.S. nuclear submarine directly ahead. Estimated range 1000 meters."

Ji smiled and thought to himself. Maybe Captain Park knew something, and the maverick submarine captain is hiding inside North Korean waters. Very clever, but not clever enough.

On Pittsburgh, Drake and Carla reentered Control. Karen was already at the fire control panel and the COB had the dive. Drake whispered to Carla, "Weps, silently man battle stations torpedo."

The ship having been rigged for ultra-quiet, phone talkers were on all levels of the ship to minimize the need to use electronic communications that might be heard outside the ship.

Carla nodded and told the Control phone talker, "Silently man battle stations torpedo." The phone talker repeated back to Carla what she had said, then in his mouthpiece he said, "Silently man battle stations torpedo."

Pittsburgh had done this hundreds of times, but never for real. In different areas of the ship, phone talkers on each level went around and silently passed the word to man battle stations. Throughout the ship crew members got out of their bunks or stopped what they were doing and quietly moved to their battle stations throughout the ship. When they got there, they broke out the appropriate damage control gear and ran fire hoses. In Control, crew members quietly entered, manned sound-powered phones, and manned their stations at the fire control panels, geographic plot and the ships control station. In the Torpedo Room, men and women entered, manned sound power phones, and prepared to fire port and starboard upper tubes. The remaining personnel gathered in the mess deck and engineering to support damage control efforts.

Drake took his favorite position, arms crossed, left hand on chin, just to the left of the XO who was behind the forward fire control panel. He looked at the ship's control party. "All stop."

The phone talker said, "All stop," into the mouthpiece.

Turning to Karen, Drake said, "Let's see what our boy does now."

Outside the ship, Pittsburgh propeller slowed as the main turbines no longer received propulsion steam. With Pittsburgh forward motion slowing, the North Korean submarine slowly came up Pittsburg's port side.

In the North Korean submarine, the XO took a report. "Captain, Sonar lost contact with the U.S. submarine."

Ji nodded his acknowledgement and thought a minute. "That means he may have opened. Go active with a single ping."

The XO wanted to say he might have detected us, but he kept quiet. He relayed the order to Sonar. Shortly a single sonar ping was heard transmitting from the ship.

The XO listened to his headset. "Captain, sonar has multiple returns. Best estimate is the U.S. submarine is 1000 meters on our starboard bow."

Ji was delighted he had done the impossible. The entire North Korean fleet had been unable to find this Pittsburgh and now he had him. "XO, direct Sonar to send the acoustic contact report with our location."

On Pittsburgh, all eyes were on the sonar displays. Karen reported. "Captain, Sonar has gained spherical passive broadband contact on the North Korean submarine, coming out of our port baffles, bearing 351. I'm setting range 1000 yards."

No sooner than Drake had acknowledged, when a loud single active sonar ping was heard. Drake was looking at the sonar display and saw the brightening. "Well, our boy knows we're here."

As Karen entered the parameters for the contact, Carla put in initial parameters for a torpedo. A minute later, a deafening four-frequency sliding sonar transmission was heard through the Pittsburgh's hull. Throughout the Attack Center people recognized this was for real.

Drake knew the significance of that transmission. "Whoa! That was no doubt a contact report. Not only does he have us, he just let his friends know where we are. He's going to have lots of help really quick."

Karen had her solution ready. "If he has friends coming, he's going to try and open fast."

Carla had moved in front of the UUV control laptop. "Captain, I can get one of our UUVs to close that guy and give us real-time video contact info if he opens range."

Drake responded, "Good idea, Weps. Do that." He then looked at the helm. "Ahead one-third, come left, steer course 087." Drake was thinking about the immediate danger this submarine posed. "XO, I worry about our boy shooting a torpedo at us. We're going to snuggle in really close."

On the North Korean submarine, the XO moved over next to the captain. "Captain, recommend we shoot one torpedo at the U.S. submarine, then quickly open range to let Commodore Park finish him off."

Ji nodded his head in affirmation. "Exactly what I was thinking. XO, fire on the U.S. submarine."

The XO not only operated the fire control panels, but also

the weapons control panel. He manipulated the solution, then adjusted the parameters to the torpedo. He finally pushed a button and there was a loud rush of air noise as a torpedo was pushed out of a bow-mounted torpedo tube. Once the torpedo was away, Ji ordered, "Ahead full, left full rudder steady, course north."

By the time the torpedo left the torpedo tube, Pittsburgh had closed to within four hundred yards of the North Korean submarine and was well within any minimum enable her torpedo might have. The minimum enable is to prevent a torpedo from turning and coming back and attacking the shooter. The torpedo ran toward Pittsburgh that was now just forward of its starboard bow. A burst of cavitation came from the North Korean submarine's propellers and they rapidly started to turn faster, generating cavitation bubbles.

On Pittsburgh, the torpedo launch was heard through the hull. The sonar supervisor called out, "Torpedo in the water, bearing 290." At the ship's control station, the helmsman started to ring up speed. The COB puts his hand down on his shoulder and nodded to him not to order increased speed.

Drake knew they were operating out of normal conditions and announced, "No torpedo evasion. Everyone stands fast. We are well inside his minimum attack range."

Karen, normally cool under any condition, was sweating profusely. "God, I hope so."

The North Korean torpedo took a right turn toward the Pittsburgh. With Pittsburgh so close, it was not able to "see" it. It went right over the Pittsburgh and then circled back in a reattack pattern, going back over Pittsburgh the other direction, but again it could not see Pittsburgh. As it passed over Pittsburgh the second time it

177

started moving aft the North Korean, went into active search mode and traveled off to the west.

As the North Korean submarine increased speed and headed north, it passed under a Pittsburgh UUV. Carla, at the UUV laptop controls, saw this. "Captain, UUV number two has video on the North Korean submarine bearing 003, range 1200 yards. He is moving out!"

Drake walked next to Carla. "No doubt he's getting out of Dodge before all hell breaks out here." He moved next to Karen and tapped her on the arm, and turned to the chief of the watch. "Chief of the Watch, rig ship for depth charge."

On the bridge of the North Korean flagship, Captain Park knew something had just occurred, due to the noise coming from his combat control center. Sure enough, his second in command came out and told him.

"Captain, combat reports submarine Kone-3 has detected the U.S. submarine bearing 260, range 18,000 meters."

His surprise had worked and now he knew exactly where this Pittsburgh was. He nodded to his second and spoke into the command telephone system. "Task force, change course to 260. Increase speed to full." Then he walked into this combat control center. "Provide the location to all ships in the flotilla." Then he picked up his command mike. "All ships and aircraft, fire depth bombs at the target. "

As the North Korean ships were changing course to the left, missiles were being fired off from the North Korean frigates and corvettes, dipping sonar helicopters moved out in front of the task force ships. On the surface close to Pittsburgh, three depth bombs landed, sunk and then exploded with a powerful damaging wave that emanated in all directions, including toward Pittsburgh's location.

On Pittsburgh, Sonar didn't have a chance to report the depth bombs before the effect of the explosions rocked the ship. In Control, personnel not holding on for support or strapped in and loose material from desks were flung into the air. In the galley and mess decks, food, pots and pans and crew members were thrown about. In the engine room, major piping and pumps flexed on their mounts. A seawater fitting ruptured with deafening noise, sending a blinding spray of high-pressure seawater into the space.

Drake had been holding onto the support bar next to the conn when the explosion hit. Around him everything was in shambles. The crew members who were not laid out on the deck were holding onto something to stay upright.

From the IMC speaker came the worst thing that could happen in a situation like this. "Flooding in the engine room." Everyone on Pittsburgh knew what that meant. The chief of the watch prepared to emergency blow ballast tanks, but Drake called over and stopped him.

"Senior Chief, no emergency blow. We don't want to be on the surface right now."

Things were getting noisy, as everyone was talking over everyone. Drake spoke out in a loud and authoritative voice. "Quiet in Control. On the helm, all stop." He looked at his sonar displays and ordered, "Range and bearing to the North Korean submarine."

Carla called out, "Bearing 013, range 2,900 yards opening."

Karen, having picked herself up from the deck and bleeding from a cut on her forehead, responded, "Solution ready."

Drake knew that by the time he got the fire order out, the North Korean submarine would be at his minimum enable. "Snap shot North Korean submarine - set speed medium."

FT2 Smith make the final adjustments and pushed the fire button on tube One. The torpedo ejection pump responded with its "Thuk! Thak! Shhhhhhhhh!" as it impulsed the torpedo from the tube.

Drake called out, "Firing point procedure Master Four, tube Two."

In the background Drake heard "Solution ready, weapon ready, ship ready."

Drake looked at the geo plat. "Shoot tube Two." Again, the Torpedo Ejection Pump responded with its Thuk! Thak! Shhhhhhhhh! as it impulsed the torpedo from the tube.

Outside of Pittsburgh, a torpedo shot out of the port side upper torpedo tube and sank below the ship close to the bottom; the motor started, and the torpedo sped off.

In the engineering space, the flooding was so loud no one could hear over the noise. The engineering officer of the watch reached up to a set of levers above him and moved them to the shut position. There was an audible hydraulic thump and the flooding noise stopped. The EOOW picked up his 1MC mike and transmitted, "The flooding has stopped."

In the engine room lower level, water was three feet above the deck plates and was dripping from the overhead. An unconscious watch stander was face down in the water with blood all around him. A damage control team arrived and tended to him as others look for the leak.

Drake was fighting to keep his composure. Now was not the time to show fear. Pittsburgh had developed an up angle due to the flooding in the engineering spaces, and the ship was slowly descending.

The COB, trying to keep Pittsburgh from sinking, had forgotten about the flooding. He spoke automatically, "Request speed, sir," then quickly realized his mistake. That wasn't going to happen until the engineers found and isolated the flooding. Drake ignored the request.

A new set of depth bombs entered the water around Pittsburgh and slowly descended, exploding near Pittsburgh. heir shock waves were massive, and the Pittsburgh bounced around as it slowly continued to sink. The bottom was close.

Pittsburgh's torpedo was closing on the North Korean submarine from astern. Two North Korean depth bombs entered the water just above it and descended. Pittsburgh's torpedo hit the submarine and two North Korean depth bombs exploded simultaneously. A massive internal explosion from the submarine and the two depth bomb detonations generated a gigantic thrust of water upward and a huge shock wave moving outward.

When the shock hit Pittsburgh, it caused a huge jerk on its hull causing the 8,000-ton nuclear submarine to roll and twist. Everyone in the Attack Center was lifted off their feet and their seats. Drake lost his handhold and was thrust into a fire control panel, severely cutting his head and knocking him unconscious. Karen, who was standing just aft of Drake, was lifted off the deck into the overhead and she fell toward Drake. As Drake hit the deck, Karen fell on top of him, and Pittsburgh hit the bottom.

The North Korean attack continued, but the intensity had slowed significantly since the explosion from the North Korean submarine. With blood oozing from her scalp, Karen pushed herself up off the unconscious Drake. Seeing his injuries, she broke down. She had never seen her captain totally unable to function, not to mention all of the damage around her.

She called out, "Get the Doc up here now." Panicking, she screamed again, "Get the Doc up here now!"

The COB came over and pulled Karen off Drake. "XO, you've got to regain your composure. The Captain can't go out and calm the crew like he always does when things turn to shit, and right now someone has to get the water out of the ship and the spaces back under control."

Karen's fear and emotional tears gave her a spaced-out look. The COB shook her and got her attention. "XO, did you hear me?"

Karen looked up and nodded as Doc arrived. Karen stood. "COB, I heard you. You take the forward spaces. I'll help the engineers get the water out."

Doc had dropped to the deck and was looking at Drake's bloody gashes and misshapen arm. She looked up, "XO, COB, I need to reset his dislocated arm and shoulder. I need you to hold him down, so he doesn't move while I reset it."

Karen and the COB both held and pressed down on Drake's upper torso. Doc moved the captain's arm vertically off the floor, then, putting her foot on Drake's shoulder, she vertically jerked his arm. Karen watched as the misshapen arm and shoulder physically moved back into a normal position.

Doc moved down and slowly manipulated Drake's shoulder. "Good, that's out of the way. I need people to get the captain into his stateroom."

Karen asked, "Should we use the mess decks or the wardroom? They're set up for medical emergencies."

Doc gave Karen a frustrated look and in an annoyed tone responded, "XO, all the tables in the mess decks and the wardroom are or will be filled with injured. My teams are working them, and the captain will be better off in his own bunk."

Karen realized she was out of line and had touched a nerve on the best corpsman she had ever served with. "Doc, I'm sorry."

The COB called over to the Ship's Control Party and into Sonar. "Seeing we're sitting on the bottom, you all are assigned to Doc. Do whatever she needs."

Karen looked around the control room area. She put her arm on the COB's shoulder. "Thank you. I needed that. Sitting on the bottom is the best thing we can do now. The North Korean's will never detect us. I'm heading aft. Let's get back to some normalcy."

Back on the North Korean flagship, Captain Park was worried his attack might not be progressing as well as he imagined it in his dreams. They had saturated the location from the contact report with depth bombs and there was no way the American nuclear submarine could have survived. Then, on the horizon in the direction of the attack a huge geyser of water erupted out of the water and he felt the low rumble of an explosion.

His combat control speaker reported, "Captain Park, Sonar holds a large explosion on the bearing to the U.S. submarine. It was an explosion and not just a depth bomb."

Sung Park smiled with delight. He had been given a chance and he had redeemed himself. He immediately went to his communication panel and called Admiral Ryu. Jong Song was in the room with him. In jubilance he reported. "Admiral, Captain Drake Chandler and his submarine USS Pittsburgh are no longer among the living."

At that moment, the combat control center called out, "Torpedo in the water!"

Ten seconds later an explosion erupted below the Najin-class frigate, Chungnam. The middle of the ship rose like two shutters on a window opening. The ship cracked in half with the forward and aft parts of the ship drifting apart.

Chapter 25

As Pittsburgh lay on the bottom, there was an eerie silence throughout the ship. Many of the crew lay on the deck severely wounded, and several were dead. Doc Rothlein had set up triage stations in the mess decks. All of the tables were now full of bleeding and groaning men and women. Most of the wounded had concussions, severe gashes, and broken bones from being thrown into sharp-edged machinery. She had set up teams of mobile crew members into triage teams to find wounded and get them stable until she could get to them.

Karen had quickly gone to the engineering spaces and proudly watched as the engineers quickly found and isolated flooding, allowing restoration of cooling sea water for the electrical generation turbines. The electrical operators and damage control teams quickly isolated problems to allow returning most of electrical services throughout the ship.

As she went down the ladder to the lower level, she walked into four feet of water above the deck plates. Lieutenant Tom Dawson and Senior Chief Reynolds were directing their teams in the fore and aft ends, restoring equipment. Chief Reynolds saw Karen and came over.

Karen spoke first. "How it's going, Chief?"

He responded, "Well, the water level is finally going down. We had to isolate several pumps and systems powered from the starboard busses. Petty Officer Markem told me his electricians have isolated the electrical components that have caused the problem. He hopes to have that correct in the next four hours."

As Karen walked through the space, she saw two sailors holding someone by the ankles who was hanging over outboard piping. "Jones, what's going on?"

Petty Officer Jones looked over his shoulder and saw Karen. "XO, tough to talk right now, ma'am, but there are some small critical sensing lines that have separated. We can't get to them, so we got Walters to get out there and repair them."

Karen smiled, having done that herself back when she was a junior officer on Michigan. Walker was a 98-pound female machinist mate and welder. Her weight and slimness made her the ideal person to have hanging out over the outboard systems to repair piping.

When Karen finally left engineering, she thought about the U.S. nuclear submarine industry. This experience had shown her that they certainly lived up to their reputation. Most ships would have never survived that attack.

Doc was having some trouble hiding her fears and anxiety as she tended Drake in his stateroom. This was the first time she had sat in over twelve hours. The Captain had been down for over eighteen hours and never really slept.

She had cleaned and dressed his many wounds and was updating his chart when he started waking up. He lifted his head, opened his eyes, saw Doc, then fell back into sleep. She was concerned. Something serious was going on here and she didn't know what it was. This was the man she depended on to take care of her and her shipmates, and now he might be dying.

There was a knock on the door and the COB entered. His uniform was damp, tatted, and filthy. "Doc, how's he doing?"

Doc looked over her shoulder. "He has several wounds, lacerations and bruises all over. He comes in and out of consciousness, but it's this deep cut on his forehead that I'm worried about."

Doc felt she was going to lose it emotionally, so she forced a smile on her face. "COB, is that the new style submarine uniform? They keep changing them so often, I was just wondering."

The COB laughed at the joke. "No. It's pretty bad out there, but the ship is coming back together. How's the rest of the crew?"

Doc put her chart down. "I've got eight dead and twenty in pretty bad shape, and the rest are patching themselves up as best they can." At this point, Doc broke down and tears started coming from her eyes as she fought to keep them in. In a quivering voice she asked. "COB, now that we're off the bottom, are we going home?"

The COB put his hand on her shoulder in a comforting, fatherly way. "I don't know."

In the wardroom, Karen was holding a meeting. Carla, the COB, the operations officer, John Walker, the engineer, the supply officer, and the communicator, sat or stood around the table. They were all dazed, in sweat-encrusted and blood-soaked uniforms, all with bandages of some sort on their heads. There was major damage everywhere. Cabinets had broken off bulkheads and non-secured items had acted like missiles, slamming into walls and doors, leaving holes or huge scars.

Karen thought of what remained of her crew. Now that the captain was out of commission, she had assumed command, and she needed to get everyone on the same page so they could plan of the next steps.

"With the captain down, I have assumed command. I have decided Pittsburgh will return to Guam ASAP."

This comment shocked Carla. "XO, you can't do that. My

God, the North Koreans are preparing to launch a nuclear attack on our country." Then, to make her point, she challenged, "Captain Chandler would never do that!"

Karen wasn't surprised at this response. "Captain Chandler is no longer in command. We've informed all the appropriate parties of that situation and we were told to depart. With what just happened I intend to do that."

The COB, who was standing rather than sitting, spoke up. "XO, I have to agree with the Weps. We are talking about a nuclear attack."

In Drake's stateroom, YN1 Tubbs was sitting with the captain, reading a three-year-old copy of People magazine. Doc was worried and wanted the captain watched around the clock. Tubbs heard the captain stir and Drake suddenly jolted out of a deep sleep and jumped to his feet, almost knocking Tubbs off his chair.

Drake was confused but seemed to be regaining some sense of awareness. "Tubbs, where is everybody?"

Tubbs was concerned and thought of calling Doc. "Sir, they're in the wardroom."

On hearing this, Drake immediately departed. Tubbs chased behind him. "But – but – sir, the Doc said you needed to stay down."

As Drake prepared to go the middle level he turned to Tubbs. "You tell the Doc that's not going to happen."

In the wardroom, a small battle of wills had erupted. Karen felt like a one-armed paper hanger fighting off Carla and the COB. The rest of the group were spilt half and half.

Karen raised her voice. "My God, have any of you walked the ship recently? It's a disaster. We maybe off the bottom, but we're lucky to be alive."

The COB had never taken on the exec like he had the captain. He trusted Drake Chandler and knew he expected COB to be frank even when it was painful. "Ma'am, pardon my French, but, ma'am, your actions are denigrating the one person in this fucking Navy who stood up for you when your career was headed for the toilet."

This comment pissed off Karen and she stood to challenge the COB. "Don't give me that crap. I know my responsibility –"

She didn't get to finish as at that moment the wardroom door burst open. Drake entered in blood-soaked khakis and head dressing. The Doc was right behind him.

Drake, in pain and frustration, turned to Doc. "Doc, I need something that controls pain but doesn't make me groggy. Now get out of here." He then shut the door in her face.

Drake turned to the table. Everybody looked astounded. Karen tried to say something, but Drake wavered her off. "We are not letting the North Koreans attack the United States!"

Karen was ready for this battle and started to make her case, even if it got her fired. "Captain, you are in no condition to make that call."

Drake looked at Karen and Carla. "XO, why did I go out and recruit you two to Pittsburgh?"

Karen was stunned at the question, and she looked at Carla who for once was also without words. She questioned Drake. "What?"

Drake asked again, "Why did I recruit you?" He saw they were not getting it. "I brought both of you to the Pittsburgh because we were the test platform for the submarine Anti-Ballistic Missile Defense system."

Karen reacted. "Sir, that was over two years ago and the program got cancelled."

189

Drake nodded. "Canceled yes, but not until we fired three successful missiles."

The COB was having trouble seeing where this was going. "Yes, sir, but how is that going to help?"

At that moment Carla got it and blurted out. "They never took the last two missiles off the ship! There are two Raytheon SM-3 modified BMD missiles in vertical tubes five and six!"

The COB shook his head. "True, but we don't have the software."

Karen now saw where this was going. "Yeah, we do, COB. When the program was shut down, they got rid of all the funding as soon as possible. They never gave us permission to return the software and our special launching components. In fact, the Raytheon and Northrop people we incredibly happy we kept everything with us."

Carla spoke up. "Captain, we'll never get all of the alignment and testing done. It took us over three days last time."

Drake acknowledged, "XO, there's testing that is necessary and testing that we can overlook. You know what that is."

Karen, who just a moment ago was on one side of this issue, now saw herself being pulled back in. "That's right, and we have everything we need."

The COB had been thinking and asked a pertinent question. "I hate to rain on anyone's parade, but we don't have any ABM SPY-1 radar to support our missiles."

John Walker spoke up. "Actually, COB, we do. The ABM ships that were pulled off to the North Korean coast are still out there, out of missile range, but the SPY-1 radars are still working. I've been watching the radio traffic and they will be monitoring the North Korean missile test."

Drake chimed in, "Those SPY-1 radars will pick up and track our missile and direct them into the North Korean missile."

Karen had initially been thrilled when she thought of using the ABM system, but then her Spock-like processes kicked in. "But, Captain, the ship's in no shape to fight. I've walked the ship and there is heavy damage everywhere. We've been ordered to depart the area. I've laid out plans to return to Guam."

Drake knew what Karen was doing. She was laying out what should normally be done. "XO, I know where you are coming from, but although I've pushed limits, I've always tried to do the right thing my whole Navy career."

Karen tried to speak. "But, Captain!"

Drake moved over to the countdown clock he had started the day before. It read 12:03:46. He turned to the group. "Allowing a North Korean nuclear attack on the United States and taking no action is immoral."

Karen knew she had lost the battle and in the back of her mind she was glad Drake had come to her rescue. She couldn't have lived with herself if she had not tried to stop the North Korean attack. "Captain we only have twelve hours until the North Koreans launch."

Drake knew he had won a tough battle. "Twelve hours, and lots to do."

Throughout the ship, activity picked up. When things are tough, it's always best to have a focused mission to get your crew working well. In the torpedo room, the connectors were made up to the ABM missile in tubes Five and Six, and checked with fire control.

In fire control, Karen supervised the installation of the ABM software. She had taken the original test documents and cut-and-pasted installation, alignment and testing procedures, which the FTs were closely following.

One hundred miles to the east, Captain Ned Parks, commanding officer of guide missile cruiser USS Lake Erie, CG-70, sat in his chair on the bridge. He was looking out at the small group of ships under his command. They were all ballistic missile defense ships that had been pulled off the North Korean coast three months earlier. For the last month, they had been cruising in the Sea of Japan watching North Korea. Bill thought to himself, *I hope we are doing something important here because this is about as boring as it gets.*

His weapons officer, Lieutenant Commander Ron Wellings, came up to him with his daily report on the ABM weapons system.

"Well, Weps, are we ready to track the North Korean missile launch tomorrow? I want no screw ups."

Ron Wellings was a fast-tracked, up and coming young officer, and he was happy to have Ned Parks as his CO. He had been in three different military engagements throughout his career including at his last command on a destroyer. If things went south, it was reassuring having a commanding officer like Captain Parks.

"Captain, our systems are all set for tracking the North Korean missile test. I have been watching the various communications and the missile test looks like it will be at about 0900 tomorrow."

Ned Parks had been impressed with young Wellings' development, and he took his daily report and started reviewing it. "I've been on satellite voice comms from CincPacFlt, ComSeventhFlt and ComThirdFlt all morning. They are really sweating blood about us being able to track that North Korean missile test." Ned looked out to sea with a sarcastic grin. "Like we can do anything. Since those admirals almost lost their jobs because they challenged the president's "Peace in our Time" initiative, they've been on real pins and needles. I can't see anything happening, but, man, are they nervous."

On Pittsburgh, Drake and Karen were in Radio observing efforts to repair the various equipment. Chief Belt, the communicator, along with John Walker and what was left of his team, were working to get equipment back up.

Petty Officer Teacher had been killed when he fell down a hatch and hit his head on machinery during the attack. Drake felt guilty because he had no time for concern over Teacher's death.

Drake knew he was lucky to have Chief Rita Belt on board. She had been a rock star in her community and had developed the new "C" school curriculum for the ET Radioman – Submarines. She had written him and asked if he would help get her to Pittsburgh. Karen had taken care of that for him.

As they walked over, Chief Belt reported. "Captain, everything went down during that attack. I hope to have at least the VLF and one SAT-comm up in about three hours. We've been able to receive but it will be a long time to get a transmitter up and I'm not sure how the antennas fared."

Karen was looking at the patch panel. "What's the status of the comms modem?"

Rita Belt smiled. "We were lucky. They went down when the power was lost but their strappings to the desk kept them from being to be jolted. One of the spook team members and Sanchez got it up and working. It's providing live video feed from the North Korean launch site."

Drake and Karen walked over and observed the video of the Tonghae Satellite Launching Ground. A North Korean missile was on a pad being serviced. Karen was concerned. "Do you think that's the missile?"

Chief Belt pulled out a secret manual on North Korean weaponry. "I've been looking at pictures of the various North Korean missiles and I think that is a Taephon-D. We're going to be able to watch and listen in real time."

This made Karen uncomfortable. "Captain, this is for real."

Drake sat drowsing in his chair on the conn. They were less than ninety minutes from the North Korean missile launch. Things had gone well. There were some problems in the testing, but the FTs and TMs had figured out ways around them. In some ways it had gone too well. This always bothered him when he was not hearing that there were problems on the ship. It usually meant people were not challenging themselves in looking for problems. But in this case, so much was broken and not operational that maybe he had become immune to reports.

Drake had tried to get a nap in the afternoon, but he could not sleep. He had got up and walked to engine room lower level and sat. There was something comforting about the sound of running machinery. Today, this included a briny smell of sea water, but still the peaceful noise of constant running machines soothed him.

Carla and two very tired looking FTs were closing up the fire control panels. Carla had been with them the whole time. Even though she didn't understand the intimate details of what they were doing, she had made sure the systems were working.

John Walker and Karen entered Control from Radio. They didn't see Drake slumped in his chair and Karen jumped when Drake spoke.

"XO, how confident are you that your testing protocols are

valid?"

Karen recovered from her fright. "It's not the most perfect set of tests, but it checked out the key elements of the fire control system needed to support launch and integration with the SPY-1 radars."

Carla had overheard the conversation and came up, proudly proclaiming, "Captain, XO, our tests and checks are completed and completed satisfactorily except for an intermittent problem with the missile tube Five."

Drake gave a quiet, "Very well."

Karen questioned Carla. "But Weps, we lost continuity to both missiles during the testing."

Carla shook off the challenge. "XO, we've addressed those problems. The weapons system is ready to support submarine BMD SM-3 missile launch."

After enjoying the banter between Karen and Carla, Drake reached out and picked up the 1MC microphone. "All hands, this is the captain speaking. In ninety minutes, the North Koreans will be launching a nuclear weapon at the United States. As you all know, destruction of that weapon is critical to the safety of the United States and the world."

Here Drake paused a beat. "It's going to get very dicey in the next two hours. I'm confident that we are trained and capable to shoot down that nuclear missile. I am also proud to be your commanding officer and I know we will prevail."

Drake put the mike back and Karen whispered in his ear. "I think the 'we will prevail' is a bit optimistic."

Drake gave her a tough-love look. "Does it matter?"

Karen shrugged. "No, it doesn't."

The COB entered Control holding three plastic balls. Drake stood up and looked. "Captain, we went through all of the dead crew member's lockers and look what we found."

Drake picked up one of the balls.

The COB looked at Karen. "I think they're radio frequency locator beacons." Drake turned the one held over in his hand and handed it to Karen.

Karen commented, "Let me guess, they were in Seaman Ames' locker."

The COB shook his head. "No, actually they were in Petty Officer Teacher's locker."

Karen was shocked. "The spook team guy?"
John Walker came over and looked at the beacons. "My God. Teacher was one of my best guys. He was with me in North Korea, and he worked 24/7. Interesting. He told me that he had talked to NSA Director Susan Grains and her assistant Michele Park just before we got on the tug to come out here." John chuckled. "While we were in North Korea, in spite his 24/7 work schedule, he and Ms. Park were always together. I think they might be related."

Karen raised her eyebrows. "Do you think they are spying for the North Koreans?"

Chapter 26

In the Situation Room, Michele Park was setting out the satellite images and transcripts of North Korean intercept messages discussing the attack and sinking of a U.S. nuclear submarine. There was concern that after the message to Pittsburgh demanding it depart immediately, they had heard nothing. Then the Navy and intelligence communities had picked up a major North Korean anti-submarine warfare operation just off their coast right in the area where the USS Pittsburgh should have been departing. This coincided with the timing of the satellite images and radio transcripts.

In her office, Susan pondered what had happened. Deep in her heart, Susan felt guilty that this Drake Chandler and his submarine crew had lost their lives, but then that's what you get for disobeying orders. And *my* goddamn order. They had got what they deserved. They might have undone all the work done to achieve the president's "Peace in Our Time" legacy.

So far Susan and the chief of staff had been able to keep a lid on the sinking of Pittsburgh. When a few press members had called for confirmation, she was able to convince them there was nothing to it. After all, United Nations confirmation of the "Peace in Our Time" initiative was currently scheduled in two weeks. With the exception of the Wall Street Journal and those assholes at FOX News, the media were fully on President Jefferson's side. They would do nothing that might make him look bad or, in this case, impact his foreign policy achievements. She would need the media in order to push for the Nobel Peace Prize. But now she had to face the ugly old men in the Cabinet and Pentagon who always second-guessed her.

As she entered the Situation Room, around her all the usual suspects waited. She saw real concern on their faces. She had to make her case for the United States to do nothing in confronting a group of people who had narrow nationalistic views of the world and not the inclusive view of a globalist international diplomacy and the new world order. Even though they supported the president's initiative, they would now revert to their cold war mentalities.

Secretary of Defense Tom Reynolds took the first shot. "Susan, I think you got the USS Pittsburgh sunk."

This was quickly validated by Admiral Rentner. "Madam Director, forcing Pittsburgh to communicate in water so close an enemy coastline is extremely dangerous."

Susan was not about to take this. "Don't give me that crap, Admiral. Much more is at stake than one submarine. We are talking about total world peace." Although Rentner was on her side, she needed to reign him in a bit. "Your man Chandler might have destroyed any chance to make that happen."

She then challenged the individuals in the room and those coming in on video conference. "Any of you that think directing USS Pittsburgh to depart was the wrong decision, I recommend you get your letters of resignation ready, so the president can sign them tomorrow."

No one in the room or on the conference was ready for that and they knew any further challenges to Susan would be the kiss of death.

Susan continued. "We don't know if anything happened to USS Pittsburgh even though these messages and intelligence data are quite detailed." Susan reemphasized, "We don't actually *know* what happened. We will wait and discuss this in two days."

All in the room were concerned their positions were all in jeopardy. They all put their heads down and acquiesced.

Chapter 27

Drake paced in his stateroom, not wanting the crew to see his fear and secretly hoping Washington would relent and send the ABM cruisers and destroyers back to the North Korean coast. The last sixty minutes had gone slowly, and he needed to prepare his ship to execute the most dangerous preemptive military action initiated by the United States since the Battle of Lexington that started the Revolutionary War.

Drake left his stateroom and entered Control. The countdown clock showed 00:09:11. Although not announced, almost everyone was at their battle stations, knowing the order was imminent. Drake looked right to the chief of the watch. "Man battle stations missile."

The chief of the watch repeated back the order and announced over the 1MC, "Man battle stations missile!" He then pulled the general alarms lever. "Gong…gong…gong…gong!" reverberated throughout the ship. The few people who were not at their stations came into Control quickly and took up their stations, apologizing for being late.

Karen was at the geo plot, looking at the topography of the North Korean shore line and making sure the plot coordinator knew the point she needed to line the periscope on.

Carla stood between her two FTs, manning the weapons control panels. The COB was on the dive. Drake took his favorite location, arms folded and left hand on cheek, between the conn and the geo plot.

The COB was the first to break the quiet. "Well, Captain, looks like we're getting a chance to shine."

Drake gave him a dirty look. "Yeah, but no matter what happens we might come out the loser here."

The COB tapped the stern planes operator on the shoulder and whispered, "Zero bubble." The young petty officer had a tremble in her hands and slowly made the adjustment.

The COB turned to look at Drake. "Well, Captain, that's why you wear that command star."

Drake smirked, smiled, and rubbed the command star on the right breast pocket of his uniform. "Thanks a lot, but right now it seems awfully heavy."

The engineer had the deck, and he came up next to Drake. "Captain, the ship is manned for battle stations missile."

Drake commented. "Very well." He moved over by the fire control panels and ordered, "XO, take the conn. Eng, maintain the deck. Weps, take over as fire control coordinator." He looked up into the radio live microphone speaker. "Radio, have you got live video feed?"

Chief Belt's voice came back over the speaker. "Yes, sir. Video feed from the launch site shows the North Korean missile is fully ready for launch."

Karen moved past Drake and went onto the conn, taking the periscope from the engineer. She called out, "Quartermaster, best bearing to Musudan-ri."

A formal replay came quickly. "Musudan-ri bears 349.6."

Drake watched his well-trained crew go through the formal mechanics of missile launch. He directed, "XO, come around to that bearing and let us know when you see rocket exhaust."

The ESM operator's voice came over the open conn speaker. "Conn ESM, picking aircraft radars. They are definitely North Korean helos and appear to be hovering off the coast."

Drake responded for Karen, who was on the scope. "Very well."

Karen did her mental calculation as she looked out the scope. "Captain, when we launch, those aircraft will definitely pick up the disturbance in the water and the rocket exhaust plume. We don't stand a chance."

Drake nodded to himself. "We've got a chance with some luck on our side."

The COB saw nervousness mounting as the battle stations missile party heard this. He announced for all to hear. "Captain, the Pittsburgh crew is all the luck we need."

On hearing that, Drake teared with pride as he ordered, "Firing point procedures, ballistic missile defense SM-3 missiles in tubes Five and Six."

As Carla watched her fire control technicians make final checks and inputs to the fire control panels, two green ready lights turned red.

In the torpedo room at the vertical launch station, TM1 Pender and Lieutenant Bruce Stubbs were making their final checks. As they did so, two green lights went out and were replaced by red. Petty Officer Pender announced into his sound-powered phone. "Weapons, VLS station, we just lost connectivity to both missiles."

As soon as he received a reply, Pender dropped onto the floor under the VLS panel and put his hands into the cabinet from the bottom.

In Control, the countdown clock showed 00:03:49. Carla had just heard the report. She ripped off the sound-powered handset and took off to the torpedo room, calling out, "Captain, we've lost inputs to the SM-3 missiles at launcher! I'm heading for the torpedo room."

With a calm apprehension and a look of concern Drake took in the report. "Very well."

FT2 Smith observed his synchronization lights with missile Five and Six were lost. As he turned to report, he realized Carla was gone. He called out to Karen. "XO, we've just lost sync with the launcher. What are they doing down there?"

Karen came off the scope and looked at the firing panel. "I don't know, but get behind your panel and make sure your boards are seated."

Smith quickly left and went behind the control panel.

For the first time, sweat showed on Drake's face as he tried to control his emotions.

Chief Belt came over the radio room speaker. "Conn, Radio, the North Koreans have started their last-minute countdown."

Karen realized she had been diverted to the weapons problem and got back on the periscope. "Captain, we've got to get the system ready. We have two minutes after any launch to get our missiles out of our tubes."

In a gut-wrenching calm Drake replied. "XO, I know. Our people are trained and doing the best they can. We follow the process."

Carla arrived at the VLS launcher panel and quickly dropped down next to Petty Officer Pender. She saw him desperately trying to reconnect two cables, but his large fingers prevented him from holding the cables and making a connection. She calmly grabbed the cable from Pender, pulled a hair from her head, spit onto the frayed wires, wrapped the hair follicle around the two frayed ends, making a tight and smooth connection. She gave it back to Pender. "Try it now."

As he reconnected the cable, Lt. Bruce Stubbs, the torpedo

officer, blurted out. "That's it, we've got a green light!

In the attack center, the countdown clock showed 00:00:45. Over the open mike, Chief Belt announced, "Conn, Radio, the North Korean missile support struts have fallen away, and it looks like the final launch sequence has started."

The engineer, Frosty Allen, started to break down. "Captain, what are we going to do?"

At that moment, Carla came back into Control and started putting on her headset. The countdown clock was at zero and holding. "Captain, launcher found and repaired a loose guidance cable in the back of the panel. Vertical launcher is ready."

Petty Officer Smith returned from the back of the weapons control panel, took his seat, pushed two buttons, and turned a switch. All missile indicators turned green. He said "Lt. Kelly, regained sync with the launch panel. Fire control panel ready."

"Very well."

Sweating profusely and smiling Carla turned to Drake. "Captain, weapons system ready." Drake was relieved and turned his head to Carla. "You seem to like cutting things close."

Throughout the ship, the sound-powered phone talkers were keeping the crew apprised of what was going on. Intense concern showed on all their faces. They had done this hundreds of times but always in the trainer or during an at-sea exercise. Never for real.

In the attack center, the ESM chirps of screeches from airborne radars increased in volume and frequency. Over the conn open mike, the report came. "Conn, ESM, three aircraft radars have shifted to sector scan. I think they have us."

Karen remained calm throughout the chaos that was omnipresent in the final minutes. "Captain, I hold a glow and exhaust fumes on bearing 349."

That was what Drake was waiting for. "Very well. Fire control insert bearing 349." Drake paused about five seconds. "Fire vertical launch missiles Five and Six."

Carla responded, "Fire vertical launch missiles in tubes Five and Six, aye." She watched Petty Office Smith press the fire Five button.

Outside on the forward deck of Pittsburgh, a starboard missile hatch opened, and a missile ejected out of the tube through the fifteen feet of water. It broke the water surface, the rocket motor lit off and the missile started to ascend. Karen had rotated the periscope to observe the missile launch and calmly announced, just like in the trainers, "Missile breaking clear of the water, rocket motor ignition, missile ... Un, Uh." Fear and excitement came into her voice. "Holy shit, it's spinning out of control!"

She watched in shock as the missile turned back toward Pittsburgh and exploded right over the water surface. The missile explosion caused a deafening noise and rocked the ship. It was certainly not as violent as the North Korean attack, but crew members had to hold on to keep from falling.

This explosion caused a breakdown in the attack center. Noise levels increased as everyone talked. Drake moved to the center of the attack center area and harshly announced, "Quiet in control!" With a calm demeaner he continued, "Things like this happen. Continue the launch sequence."

Drake's announcement got the battle station party back on track and they quieted down. Everyone got back to monitoring their panels and operating their stations.

Eight miles to the northwest, three North Korean MI-14PL attack helicopters saw the commotion caused by Pittsburgh's failed missile launch. The helicopter team leader noted the disturbance on the horizon and the radar returns on the missile, and ordered, "All helos, missile launch bearing 143. All aircraft attack!"

On Pittsburgh, the ESM open mike announced, "Conn, ESM, all three aircraft radars have locked on and shifted to attack frequencies. Bearing 323."

Topside on Pittsburgh, the remains of the first missile were slowly descending around them. On the forward deck, the open missile hatch closed and a second hatch to the left of it opened. When the hatch locked open into place, the first ASW missile hit the water, exploding close to Pittsburgh sending up a huge splash and shock wave. Pittsburgh jerked. Seconds later, the second BMD missile ejected from a tube, broke the water surface, the rocket motor lit off and the missile started its ascent.

In Control, several crew members had been knocked off their feet, but most held on to something to stay on their feet or in their seats. Loose material had been thrown about.

Karen, with blood flowing from a gash over her eye, hung from the scope in pain. "Second missile broke clear of the water, rocket motor ignited, and missile ascending on normal profile."

Drake fought to maintain his calm. "Very well. Stay with the countdown."

One hundred miles to the east, all hell was breaking loose on USS Lake Erie. Ned Parks was on the bridge looking out to the west to observe the North Korean missile test. So far, the missile test appeared to be typical of many he had observed. His BMD weapons control center speaker erupted with an incoherent transmission about an SM-3 BMD missile launch.

The SPY-1 radar had picked up a SM-3 BMD missile

ascending and going after the North Korean missile test.

Ned Parks charged into the BMD weapon's control center. "What the hell is going on?" He pushed the radar operator away from his panel. "Shut down that goddammed missile now! Who fired that missile?" He look around, confused. "Weps, I am going to have your ass!"

In the back of the control center, the backup BMD radar operator had been tracking the telemetry of the North Korean test missile and determined that its telemetry and trajectory showed it heading for the United States. He could not get anyone's attention, so he went back to his job of tracking the North Korean missile.

Close to Pittsburgh, two ASW torpedoes were dropped into the water, their motors started, they went active and turned toward Pittsburgh. They quickly locked on and increased speed. *Ping...ping...ping...ping!* The sonar open speaker announced, "Conn, Sonar, air dropped torpedoes bearing 090. They are close." After a short pause it continued, "Conn, Sonar, torpedoes have locked onto Pittsburgh."

In the attack center, Drake could hear the active transmissions through the hull. *Ping...ping...ping...ping!* He stepped over to the ADC MK-5 panel on the conn and pushed two buttons. Aft on Pittsburgh's hull, two ADC MK-5 torpedo counter-measure devices ejected out of the lower stern area of the ship. They spun, make broad spectrum noise and released bubbles.

The North Korean torpedoes stopped pinging, turned toward the evasion devices and recommenced homing.

Drake stood, arms crossed, on the conn and coolly watched the sonar display.

After launch, Pittsburgh's BMD missile quickly settled in on its trajectory, vertically arcing toward a bright glow in the sky.

207

The SPY-1 tracking radar from the USS Lake Erie was received, synchronized, and started correcting the missile flight path to intercept the North Korean missile. The North Korean missile reached its apogee with Pittsburgh's missile coming up from behind. The North Korean rocket motor began to break away and a nuclear weapon bus started emerging from the missile payload bay.

Back in the water next to Pittsburgh, the two torpedoes attacked the torpedo evasion devices and, hitting nothing, circled back and re-locked onto Pittsburgh. Inside Pittsburgh the torpedo active pings were getting louder. *Ping...ping...ping...ping!*

In space, just as the North Korean nuclear warhead was out of its payload bay, the Pittsburgh missile moved alongside and detonated right next to the warhead. A monstrous, bright explosion followed. Multiple damaged pieces of the warhead and the warhead bus continued moving down range.

On the Lake Erie O-2 level, a warrant officer and chief petty officer were observing the missile test. They viewed a bright and loud explosion in the northeastern sky. The warrant officer leaned over to the chief. "Chief, that was one hell of an explosion. I thought that this was a test, and no one was supposed to disturb it."

The Chief looked amazed. "Man, that was some explosion! Yes, sir, that was the order, but in all the years we have been doing BMD exercises and live fires I never saw an explosion like that."

Next to Pittsburgh, the two torpedoes, even though they had locked onto the ship, started to interfere with each other. They both come within thirty feet of Pittsburgh and exploded. The shock wave was huge, but not close enough to penetrate the submarine hull.

The shock waves jerked Pittsburgh harder than the depth bombs from earlier. This time the Pittsburgh and her crew were more prepared. The explosion drove Pittsburgh down hard away from periscope depth. Pittsburgh's periscope snapped off at the top of the sail. The shock wave again threw crew members into the overhead and bulkheads, but being aware of what was coming, most of the crew were able to protect themselves.

Drake and Carla were on their knees, bleeding from new cuts on their heads and arms. Karen was laying on the deck, with broken periscope handles in her hands as she looked at Drake, stunned.

"Oh, my God, that was a huge flash! Our missile must have hit the target and caused a nuclear fizzle."

Drake nodded, "That's how it's supposed to work, so let's hope so."

Sound-powered phone reports had been coming into control and damage control central in the mess decks. The chief of the watch was unconscious, and the COB was manning the ballast control panel and was still diving officer of the watch. He looked over to the conn.

"Damage control reports from all stations. It's bad, but nothing they can't handle."

Carla got up off the floor, bloodied from cuts on her face and scalp and with one large gash on her right arm. She walked over next to the COB with her smart mouth. "Wow! Those boys and girls at EB and Newport News know how to make great submarines."

Drake was still on his knees, chuckling and shaking his

head at Carla. He turned to the quartermaster. "Take a sounding."

The quartermaster came back, "Sir, fifty fathoms beneath the keel."

Drake stood and announced, "It's time to get out of Dodge." He looked around at the damage in his control room. "Diving officer, make your depth two hundred feet. All ahead full – cavitate! On the helm, right five degrees rudder, steady course 090."

Chapter 28

At the Tonghae Satellite Launching Ground conference room, there was an atmosphere of enthusiasm. Mr. Song, Admiral Rhee, Commodore Park, and General Kyun looked outside the large windows overlooking the site holding champagne flutes in their hands. They had watched their Taypgodo-3 missile with its nuclear payload smoothly lift off and head for the United States. As it rose higher into the sky, it executed all the telemetry corrections to take its payload to hit the United States.

Suddenly, they saw on the horizon what appeared to be the exhaust glow of a rocket ascending out in the ocean. The rocket started to merge with the Taypheo-3 and two minutes later they saw a bright explosion well out into space to the east. The light from the explosion blinded them as they looked.

A look of horror came over everyone. A young lieutenant burst into the room. "Mr. Song, right after the missile launch, our ASW helicopters detected missiles coming out of the water right off the coast. They attempted to stop them and were able to sink the submarine that launched them."

Jong gave a harsh look at Admiral Rhee and Commodore Park, but then, in a surprise move, he quickly put his glass down and departed rapidly. A look of concern and shock came over the faces of those who watched him leave. A few minutes later, a stern-looking gentleman with three armed personnel entered, looking rather snarky.

"I'm looking for Mr. Jong Song. The supreme leader wants him in his palace immediately."

Chapter 29

Pittsburgh moved swiftly to the east. The crew was still at battle stations, the spaces were in disarray, but there was a sense of tired joviality coming from the Pittsburgh's crew.

Drake got up and walked over and helped a battered and crying Karen to her feet. She hugged Drake in agony and more tears flowed. "I'm sorry, I challenged your authority. I was wrong."

Drake felt a great admiration for Karen Young and hugged her like an older brother calming his troubled sister. "XO, you were just doing your job. Now we need to contact Captain East and let him know where we will be in two hours, so we can communicate."

Karen, still sobbing, looked at the periscope handles still in her hands and tried to laugh. "Maybe I can use these to get better radio reception."

Drake broke out in laughter. "I can't believe it. You pick this time to demonstrate humor." Then he got serious. "XO, get a UHF burst message ready to send to Commodore Rains that we are still alive and must meet immediately. We will be on the surface in the vicinity of Ulleungdo Island in two hours." He turned to Carla. "Weps, get us immediately to periscope depth and transmit the XO's message. Then get back down, go to flank speed and head for Ulleungdo Island."

With the message sent and Pittsburgh safely on her way to Ulleungdo Island, Drake entered his stateroom and collapsed in his chair. He had not slept in three days and the exhaustion of high-pressure vigilance and anxiety came over him. He looked up at the pictures of his wife and kids and then around his disheveled stateroom and broke down crying.

He opened his locked file drawer and pulled out his punitive letter of reprimand. He read it one more time. There was no way he would survive. He had directly disobeyed an order, then, without authority, initiated a use of force against another nation. He had thirty-seven crewmembers dead and another forty or so were injured, several of them severely. This won't be a summary court martial, this will be a full court martial, where they can send people to prison. The exhaustion finally got to him and he fell onto his desk and slept.

Chapter 30

The Ballistic Missile Early Warning System had alerted on the North Korean test missile launch, causing the National Defense Network to come to full alert. The complicating factor was the detection of the huge explosion in space just over Japan. With much of the cold war missile detection and alerting system mothballed, no one knew what was going on.

Susan Grains had gathered key military figures and the president's closest advisors in the situation room, many of them by remote video conference. Tensions ran high in the room as all these participants realized that something had happened. In Washington, D.C., those in power don't care about right or wrong but only about not being the one who gets thrown under the bus by someone protecting his or her position. Everyone in the room and on the video conference call knew this process was just starting.

President Jefferson, fundraising in San Francisco, came in on video conference from a secure location at a left-over Emergency Operating Center at the former Alameda Naval Air Station. He came into the conference extremely irate and with all guns blazing. "What in the hell is going on back there? How could we shoot down a goddamn North Korean missile test?"

Susan attempted to answer. "Sir, we were –"

She was harshly overridden by an extremely irate president with arms waving and fingers pointing. "I finally got Supreme Leader Kim on the phone. That little bastard gave me a fucking holier-than-thou speech and called me a liar for going back on my promises at our summit. He then proceeded to tell me my 'Peace in Our Time' initiative is dead."

Chief of Staff Clark James tried to placate the president. "We'll be holding a press conference to announce our apologies to Leader Kim."

The president wasn't listening as he focused in on the CNO, Admiral Gensen. "Admiral, what in the hell were you doing? I heard some BMD cruiser saw a missile come up and shoot down the North Korean test missile."

Admiral Gensen tried to respond. "Yes, Mr. President. USS Lake Erie was monitoring the North Korean test missile launch and was tracking it when a missile appeared that closed on the North Korean missile and evidently destroyed it. Sir, that could not have been us. We had no vessels in the area that could have done that."

The president was now even more infuriated. "Well, you try telling that to the supreme leader of North Korea, who says he has a video of some submarine shooting down his missile test."

This was the first time any of them had heard this accusation. Submarine Force Commander Vice Admiral Rentner spoke up. "Mr. President, as you know we had a submarine, the USS Pittsburgh, in the area, but she could not have done this."

This didn't seem to calm the president. Rear Admiral Mike Collar interjected. "But Tony, Pittsburgh was the submarine that demonstrated the submarine variant anti-ballistic missile capability."

Tom Reynolds, secretary of defense, saw the knives coming after him and spoke up in his own defense. "But the president and my predecessor shut down that program two years ago."

In his video monitor, Admiral Collar was seen leaning forward. "Yes, sir, but you never funded taking the missiles or the

215

system hardware and software off her."

At this point the president was livid. "What? You mean there was a submarine off the coast of North Korea with anti-ballistic missiles?" Distraught, he continued. "Why wasn't I told? Where in the hell is the goddamn submarine now?"

Admiral Rentner responded. "Mr. President, we don't know. Until this happened, we thought she had been sunk by the North Koreans."

Susan envisioned herself being sucked under the oncoming Greyhound and retorted, "We ordered that submarine to get out of there and they directly refused the order."

The president was totally confused. "What is this about one of our submarines being sunk? How does that happen and who the world was in charge?"

Seven thousand miles to the west, Pittsburgh was on the surface as Captain Mains and his aide were being dropped topside by a helicopter. As Ralph Mains hit the deck, he saw obvious damage to Pittsburgh's sail and hull. As he went aft, he noticed that most of the topside crew were injured, with bandages and multiple bruises and several lacerations. He quickly descended into the ship.

As he hit the lower level, Carla Kelly was there to meet him. She had a severe gash over her right eye, a large bruise on her right arm and her left arm was in a sling. "Welcome aboard, Commodore. Sorry we can't be more inviting, but not a lot of our facilities are working right now. We're gathered in the wardroom."

As Ralph walked down the center passageway and entered the wardroom, he was shocked. It was a disaster. Everyone had the same bandages, bruises and lacerations he had seen topside.

Drake and Karen were at their seats and the COB was standing behind them. Most of the key officers were sitting around the table. Ralph didn't wait for any niceties. "Captain, what did you do? All hell's breaking out. Someone shot down a North Korean missile test and the president and Admiral Rentner are on the warpath."

Drake had expected as much, but picked up on the words "missile test." This sent a shiver of fear through him as he responded. "Sir, that was no missile test. That was a nuclear attack on the United States, and we shot it down."

Ralph was now confused. "It was *what?* How in the world did you shoot that missile down?" Ralph thought minute. "Forget that. I know how you did it." He looked down in concern. "Well, that was a planned missile test and right now the North Koreans are in full diplomatic assault to challenge the United States. They are preparing to start an artillery barrage into South Korea as we speak. There are ten million people living in the Seoul area and they will be devastated."

Ralph saw astonishment in Drake's and Karen's eyes. These were two officers he most respected and realized he didn't know the whole story. "Okay, how did you know it was a nuclear attack?"

Drake was getting more worried as this discussion went on. "You remember we were mapping the continental shelf. Well, we found a festooned underwater communication cable and tapped into it."

Ralph was shocked. "You what?" He then looked at Carla. "Let me guess. Kelly brought a modem from the DevRon."

Drake nodded and responded, "And I'm not going to tell you how we did that."

Ralph was now more concerned. "You used the Submarine

217

Special Communication Network to report back, didn't you?"

Drake nodded.

"That's why I never heard any of this about the North Koreans and a nuclear attack. I'm not sure Admiral Collar did either. Rentner and those bastards in D.C. never alerted us to your concerns." Ralph continued, "The big problem now is how do we prove it was a nuclear attack. The North Koreans claim it was a missile test."

Drake's face showed for the first time he recognized his dilemma. "Commodore, in that case, we're probably screwed."

Chapter 31

The 27 MC speaker in the wardroom crackled. "Captain, Radio, established comms and received a satellite communication directing we come up on a live video conference with the White House Situation Room. I'm making those connections and will patch them into the wardroom monitors."

Five minutes later, the two wardroom video screens lit up: one a picture of the White House Situation Room; the other showing the president of the United States.

In the Situation Room, Michele entered and handed a note to Susan. Susan announced, "We have the submarine Pittsburgh coming in on video feed."

Susan and all in the Situation Room watched in horror as one of the wall monitors shifted to a picture of a small room with a table. Around it were people who looked like they had just been through a war zone. They were dirty, wearing torn uniforms, heavily bandaged and with what looked like cuts and bruises on their faces. Overhead lights hung by wires and storage cabinets had their doors hanging open.

Susan looked shocked. She called out, "On the submarine, this is the White House Situation Room. Are you online?"

Chief Belt's voice could be heard. "White House Situation Room, this is USS Pittsburgh. I am getting the last checks done this circuit."

Susan was upset that the system was not working and even more upset at these submarine sailors would dress so inappropriately when they were addressing her and the president of the United States. As soon as the video of the submarine cleared up and she saw movement, she informed the president. "Mr. President, we have video communications from USS Pittsburgh. It is patched into you and the Situation Room video link."

For most in the Situation Room, it was confusing. There were video screens everywhere, with the president on one and the submarine wardroom on another, and feeds from the Pentagon, Norfolk, Virginia, and Hawaii.

On the Pittsburgh, Drake saw the Situation Room and the president on his two monitors. "This is Commander Drake Chandler, commanding officer USS Pittsburgh on the circuit. With me is Captain Ralph Mains, Commander Submarine Group Seven."

The president still had not cooled down and the fact that the individuals were dressed in dirty rags added to his ire. "What in the world did you think you were doing, shooting down a North Korean test missile? You've caused an international incident."

Drake tried to respond. "Mr. President, the North Koreans fired a nuclear armed missile at the United –"

The president did not let him finish. "That's preposterous. You have no idea of the chaos you've caused and the potential for South Korea to be attacked at any moment."

Admiral Renter saw the intense frustration in the president's eyes. He forcefully spoke up. "Captain Mains, I want you to relieve Commander Chandler immediately."

The president's face finally softened.

Ralph was not happy with that order. He got up from his seat, moved behind Drake. Drake's head bent down in shame, but he quickly recovered, stood, and looked directly at the monitors.

"Mr. President and Admiral Rentner, no one is relieving me of my command. I just lost the lives of over thirty-seven men and women and over forty of my crew are seriously injured because someone placed a mole on my ship and made my presence known to the enemy."

An uproar developed in the Situation Room as everyone tried talking and shouting at the USS Pittsburgh monitor.

At that moment, two unused Situation Room monitors came to life with feeds from CNN. The screen showed they were broadcasting from Pleasanton, California's Upper Playgrounds. Men and women in yellow anti-contamination clothing were walking inside taped-off areas with radiation sensors. State of California, City of Pleasanton, University of California Berkley, and Livermore Laboratory vans were in the background. They were looking over a piece of metal in a small crater.

A reporter, foolishly dressed in anti-contamination clothing, while his cameraman and those around him were not, talked with CNN's Wolf Blitzer. "Wolf, we are here in Pleasanton, California, where chunks of radioactive metal have fallen into a local park. High radiation levels are being recorded and sources tell us initial responders are showing symptoms of radiation sickness." The camera showed a technician moving a Geiger counter around and over the metal piece. The meter gauge spiked to a high reading with rapid clicking. The reporter continued, "Evidently, similar pieces of metal have fallen into Paso Robles and Yosemite California. We have also received unconfirmed reports that material has fallen into parts of Alaska and Canada. We have an unconfirmed report that an immediate responder, who was a former Navy nuclear missile technician, described the radioactive pieces being like something from a nuclear warhead."

The Situation Room went coldly quiet. The president's face, that moments before was red with rage, was now pale, and he appeared shaky and slightly incoherent. "Please turn off the TV monitors."

As the president regained some composure, he addressed Drake. "You on the submarine, I'm sorry, but what's your name and what were you trying to say?"

"Mr. President, I'm Commander Drake Chandler, commanding officer, USS Pittsburgh. I was saying the North Korean missile test was not a test, but a nuclear missile launched at California."

The president's fear had now been replaced by loud frustration. "You mean you knew about this attack earlier and you didn't tell anyone?"

Everyone in the Situation Room got looks of concern on their faces. President Jefferson knew he had disrupted Drake's report. "Commander, I am sorry. Please continue."

Susan knew she was in serious trouble if she didn't stop this train before it crashed into her career as national security advisor. "Mr. President, we had no imagery! There is no way the North Koreans would do something like that."

The president was now pissed. "Susan, be quiet! Commander, please continue."

Drake spoke. "Mr. President, about two weeks ago, we intercepted a message that the North Koreans intended to launch a nuclear weapon at the United States disguised as a missile test. We immediately reported it, and no one took us seriously. Then seven days ago, we intercepted a message, including video of the launch site, stating that the target was San Francisco, and it was to go off on the Fourth of July at 2100 local time."

The president interrupted in a state of disbelief. "My God! Were they targeting me?"

Drake continued. "We informed our chain of command of this we were told to depart the area. Believing they misunderstood the gravity of what I said, I sent a very forceful message telling them I thought they were wrong, and I intended to stay on station."

The president was now engaged. "Why didn't you depart? That would have been easy."

"Sir, we started picking up more communications showing that the North Koreans had direct knowledge of what we were telling Washington. They knew we were right off their coast and that we had informed Washington about their attack."

Now the president was livid. "They *what?*"

Drake was a bit concerned with this conversation. "Based on that, I made the decision to stay and prepare our ballistic missile defense weapons for launch."

The president felt a little puzzled. "That was kind of gutsy."

Drake wasn't sure how to respond. "Mr. President, it's what I was trained to do. The CNN video feed pretty much tells what happened after that."

The president now started to put together what had happened and what he needed to do to protect himself. He knew if this story ever got out, and it would, his presidency could be destroyed. With a tremor in his voice he stated, "I can't believe something like this could happen. I had an agreement and I saw Supreme Leader Kim actually destroy a portion of his nuclear material."

He paused and looked around for someone to tell him what to say. Finally, he addressed the group. "Chief of staff, come up

223

with an action plan fast. I'm flying back immediately, and I want to take action." The president turned his video off.

The chief of staff stood and looked at Susan. "Ms. Grains, I think we need to talk in my office." He turned to the secretary of defense. "Tom, we need to get the attorney general and FBI here ASAP." Returning his attention to Susan, he said, "Ms. Grains, I think you may want to have a personal lawyer present."

With everyone else shell-shocked, the SecDef, Susan and chief of staff departed.

Those remaining in the Situation Room sat motionless with blank stares on their faces. VADM Rentner was looking around his conference room, but everyone had left.

Admiral Collar finally came in on his video feed. "Ladies and gentlemen, I recommend we end this video conference. But before we do, Captain Chandler, all of us and the entire nation owe you and your Pittsburgh crew an immeasurable debt. The loss of thirty-seven submariners is unthinkable, but you and your crew's resolve to stay and fight is a decision that not many would have made. You have saved the United States and its citizens from great harm."

Mike knew Drake was still concerned about his punitive letter. He said, "And for your information, the package sent from Captain Sails at ComSubRon Fifteen was received and immediately shredded."

Epilogue

One day later, there was great suspense as the president prepared to tell the American people about the North Korean attack. Karen and Drake were in his stateroom going over their mission report when the broadcast was received and sent to all the monitors in the ship. Drake and Karen stopped their review and watched.

Outside the White House, CNN reporter, Ted James, was set up in advance of the president's address. "Wolf, the President is expected to tell the American people what occurred last week during what was a missile test by the North Koreans. I have heard that a nuclear weapon might have been launched at the United States. But, wait. I see the president is entering the east room of the White House."

The camera in the east room came on. The president moved to the podium. There were no reporters.

"My fellow Americans, I talk to you today with a sad heart and great disappointment. As you know, my staff recently concluded an agreement with North Korea to stop their development of nuclear weapons in exchange for support from the United States. Two days ago, North Korea launched a nuclear weapon at the United States in direct violation of our agreement and Leader Kim's personal assurances that they wanted to join in my 'Peace in Our Time' initiative. Unfortunately, I was not correct in my assumption that North Korea would be a willing partner.

Not willing to totally withdraw our forces, I had directed a covert ballistic missile defense capable submarine be located off the coast of North Korea. That submarine, USS Pittsburgh, detected the nuclear launch and destroyed the missile before its payload could detonate over the United States.

"Unfortunately, some pieces of the weapon fell into northern California, several of which were highly radioactive. The fantastic response of State of California and local government first responders minimized any danger to the public. We owe them a great deal of thanks. I will have more information in the coming days and my administration will get that out as soon as possible. "I have called Leader Kim and expressed my outrage at these actions. Leader Kim has expressed his regrets and shared with me that rogue military officers in his regime conducted the nuclear launch without his knowledge. Those officers have been arrested and executed. In the meantime, I have directed my ambassador at the United Nations to bring charges against North Korea in the U.N. Security Council and subsequently the World Court. I want to thank you, the American people, for your support these last days and I know we will successfully put this behind us. God bless America."

The screen shifted back to Ted Pott. "Wolf, that was certainly direct. I understand members of Congress have started an investigation into this incident and for once it has broad bipartisan support. I also understand the president's national security advisor, Susan Grains, has resigned and has taken a position as dean of Asian Diplomatic Studies at Harvard University. Also, the national security advisor executive assistant, Ms. Michelle Pak, was found dead in Rock Creek Park with her throat slit. Police are investigating."

As the broadcast ended, Drake and Karen stared to laugh. Karen blurted out, "I especially like the 'I had directed a covert ballistic missile defense capable submarine be located off the coast of North Korea.' He didn't have the faintest idea of what was going on."

Drake nodded. "How could a U.S. president let some staff members operate behind his back and not make him aware of what we found? Evidently, this Ms. Grains was part of that and then there's the coincidence of her executive assistant, the Pak woman, getting her throat slit."

Two days later, Pittsburgh was about halfway home to Guam. The crew had done a good job of cleaning up and repairing much of the minor damage. Drake and Karen were finishing their patrol report and going over a medals package in Drake's stateroom when RM2 Sanchez entered, carrying a message board.

"Message boards, sir and ma'am."

Karen reached out and took the board.

Sanchez turned to depart. Drake saw she was walking with an extreme limp. "Sanchez, great job in getting the satellite comm link back up after the missile launch. Chief Belt said you were the lead on that. Things might have been much different it you hadn't accomplished that."

A huge smile came across Sanchez's face. "All in a day's work for a Pittsburgh sailor." Realizing she might have been out of line she came back. "Sir, I'm sorry about that comment. I'm trying to be like Lieutenant Kelly, but that was inappropriate."

Drake and Karen were still smiling. Drake said, "Yes, that was a bit inappropriate. As is Lieutenant Kelly, often." He looked at Sanchez with an element of great pride. "I see you have a request in to attend the Naval Academy. I signed off on that yesterday with my highest recommendation and it will be sent as soon as we return to port. The Navy needs more Lieutenant Kellys, and she has been a great role model for you and the women on board. I just hope the Naval Academy can handle something like that."

Sanchez broke into a huge grin. "Yes, sir, I'm sure they can."

As Sanchez departed, Karen continued reading the message traffic. All of a sudden, she began to laugh. "Captain, you're not going to believe this. We're not going home to Guam. We've being rerouted to the Persian Gulf. Looks like Captain Tom Witson and his USS Illinois are in trouble."

Made in the USA
Columbia, SC
25 March 2022

58170309R00138